"A brilliant young writer. David Jay Brown writes like Walt Whitman on acid. He remembers his psychedelic experiences better than any other writer."
— Robert Anton Wilson, author of *Cosmic Trigger* and *Everything Is Under Control*.

"David Jay Brown is an ECCO agent. His writing is fantastic."
— John Lilly, author of *The Scientist* and *Center of the Cyclone*.

"David Jay Brown keeps the spirit of psychedelic literature alive with this fractal-driven, extra-terrestrial, meta-conscious, and sub-molecular adventure. If you've never had sex on acid but always wanted to, then read this book."
— Douglas Rushkoff, author of *Ecstasy Club, Media Virus*, and *Coercion*.

"I love David Jay Brown's writing."
— Timothy Leary, author of *Flashbacks* and *Info-Psychology*.

"Phantasmagoria in the fast lane."
— Oscar Janiger, M.D., author of *A Different Kind of Healing*.

"That our perfected selves whisper to us from the future is but one of David Jay Brown's fertile insights."
— Terence McKenna, author of *The Food of the Gods*.

"What if your lover's kiss could transmit a contagious, mind-altering bio-program — a psychedelic key that opens the gateway between worlds? This inventive premise infects the plot of David Jay Brown's zany rollercoaster novel *Virus*, and gives fresh meaning to the old slogan: 'Do hugs not drugs'."
— Nick Herbert, author of *Quantum Reality* and *Elemental Mind*.

Virus:
The Alien Strain

Virus:
The Alien Strain

by

David Jay Brown

NEW FALCON PUBLICATIONS
TEMPE, ARIZONA, U.S.A.

International Standard Book Number: 1-56184-144-7
Library of Congress Catalog Card Number: 99-64783

First Edition 1999

Cover art by Brummbaer

The paper used in this publication meets the minimum requirements of the American National Standard for Permanence of Paper for Printed Library Materials Z39.48-1984

Address all inquiries to:
NEW FALCON PUBLICATIONS
PMB 277
1739 East Broadway Road #1
Tempe, AZ 85282 U.S.A.
(or)
320 East Charleston Blvd. • Suite 204-286
Las Vegas, NV 89104 U.S.A.

website: http://www.newfalcon.com
email: info@newfalcon.com

TABLE OF CONTENTS

DEDICATION

For Arlen Riley Wilson

With Loving Appreciation:

Sherry Hall & Carolyn Mary Kleefeld

CHAPTER 0

A wildfire raged across her mind, and she retreated further and further away from herself to escape the heat. Upon detaching, ever-so-slightly, from the warm-blooded vehicle that she called home, expressions of inquiry began to rise up, one by one, like soap bubbles inside of her. Each question, complete with trembling punctuation mark, hung there for a moment in the pregnant void of conceptual space, as she reflected upon it. After each mystery dissolved, the next question in sequence rose up to replace it.

Questions sprouted questions, like smaller fractal forms emerging from a larger, more global pattern. Now, she thought to herself, just what was the reason that I decided to inhabit this material body in the first place? What was the point of all this? Why did I go through the enormous amount of trouble required to incarnate on this messy planet? What am I doing here? What was it that I was supposed to accomplish? Why are all these simple things so damn difficult to recall? Why? Why? Why?

Sari Feline sat staring dreamily, like a lazy cat with unfocused eyes sitting atop a warm automobile hood, trying — oh, so hard — to remember what the original inspiration for her existence was. The weave of reality had begun to unravel, and if only she could locate that lost thread, it seemed, she could figure it all out, and everything would come together and make sense again.

She deeply pondered a murky never-ending stream of sticky existential questions, not moving a muscle for hours, in a body that seemed several sizes too tight for her spirit. Although reflections flicker-flashed incessantly on the back of her retina, and neurochemical demons seemed to be persistently gnawing away on her optic nerves, the movement of images did not appear to make any impression on her seething neural tissue. She had certainly seen better days.

Sari, one of the many patients on the ward infected with the mysterious new virus, had her slender limbs now twisted up into a yogic caricature, with her arms and head held below her left leg. Her pretty Asian face looked unexpectedly radiant, housing two deep pools of shimmering obsidian. Her long straight hair dripped down from her head and over her shoulders like the jet black ink spray of an excited squid.

The muscles on her face appeared relaxed, except for the faint curl of her lips that spelled smugness. She was wearing a long blue hospital gown, no panties, and seemed oblivious to the fact that the gown was pulled up almost to her waist, revealing a dark, heavily bushed, pubic region. A television in the corner was airing a new music video. "Get Vivid!" Sari sang softly, closed her eyes, and wiggled her spirit to the rolling rocking rhythms.

"It's medication time. All west-wing patients taking medication, please come to the nurse's station," the electronically enhanced voice suddenly announced with unquestionable authority. Sari tuned her eyes through the flavors of the visible light spectrum. During the next few moments she watched as rows of different colored crayons melted together, into a flowing, multi-hued stream. The crayons became a troop of staggering psychiatric patients, draped in loose blue gowns, moving sluggishly toward the nurse's station.

She then listened to their echoes reverberating down the long hollow halls, and heard her own heart beating. There was laughter inside her head. Sari became quite alarmed when two mechanized demons, impersonating psych technicians, tried to coax her into swallowing a miniature cup filled with a rainbow assortment of pills and capsules.

"Ask for some grape juice," she whispered softly to herself. "Can I have some grape juice?" she asked a moment later in a much louder voice, concluding that she was in the company of two sinister interstellar demonoids. Reluctantly she swallowed the pills one by one, washing them down with the bitter metallic grape juice, listening to her own voice, which seemed to sing from the television like a battle cry:

Arise! Arise!
Open up your eyes!
Arise! Arise!
Everything's alive!

Sari often sat for hours without moving, frozen in rigid catatonic posture. Other times she chatted away endlessly, seemingly with herself, and would suddenly burst into a dramatic performance. When asked who she was talking to, she replied with a closed-mouthed smile, giggled, and then said shyly, "It's a secret."

The staff at the hospital had concluded that she was suffering from a psychotic break as a result of the mysterious viral infection, and was hearing hallucinatory voices. But Sari saw things differently. From her point of view, she was having a close encounter with an alien virus from outer space, and her brain was opening up to all kinds of wonderful new and exciting signals from another world.

Sari loved to dance, and did so a lot. This made her happy. She danced around the ward to a beat that was heard by no one else but her. Sometimes she drew for hours, and everyone, staff and patients alike, marveled at her intricately detailed drawings of mythological mushroom people, crystalline pixie swarms, and strange other-worldly creatures breathing birth to far stranger creatures. Sari seemed possessed.

Sometimes Sari felt very sad and lonely, like the whole universe was an empty hollow void, and no one understood her. Her family and the hospital staff thought that she was so out of touch with reality that they caged her up like a wild animal. They were all convinced that she was totally crazy. Even other patients accused her of having made a "pact with the devil," or of having a "ghost lover." This made her cry at times.

But again, let us emphasize, from Sari's perspective, the matter appears far more interesting. You see, Sari wasn't really alone. She had a friend from another world, a parallel dimension of sorts. Sari and this disembodied entity were extremely fascinated with one another, in an erotic sort of way, even though this entity didn't quite have a physical form per say, in the way that we humans know it, except in Sari's brain.

She couldn't quite figure out just what in the world this entity was, because it was most definitely not human, nor exclusively animal or plant — rather, it seemed like a hybrid of the two, a composite entity of sorts, yet ultimately beyond matter. Sari suspected that this entity was really an angel, as he would manifest to her in whatever form she most needed or fantasy she most desired — sometimes as a lover, sometimes as a teacher, sometimes as a friend. Sometimes as a master, Sari smiled, sometimes as a slave.

The entity spoke to her in the soft sweet voice of a young boy by the name of Daimon, the voice of an angel. Daimon claimed to be very ancient, originating in a star system billions of light years from earth, and that he had now evolved beyond his mere physical form. He carried with him staggering historic roots in the realm of billions of years, yet he always seemed delightfully fresh in his perspective, erotic in his style, and unquestionably hip with his sense of humor, as he overflowed with lesson-teaching mythic tales, relevant to all aspects of human affairs.

Daimon had evolutionary thrust, Sari thought with admiration, and he promised to make her rich and immortal. They were growing quite fond of one another, and an interdimensional love affair of sorts between the two was in the process of blossoming.

So on this one day, not long past the turn of the millennium, Sari was sitting quietly at a table in the dayroom, totally absorbed in conversation with her non-material playmate, while working diligently on the details of her latest drawing. She pulled her hand away momentarily to look down at the image of a huge Celtic-style mother goddess, with her legs spread open wide, giving birth to a swirling spiraling galaxy cluster of stars and eyes.

Sari knew that her alien friend liked her drawing because of the way he made her spinal cord rhythmically tingle up and down inside with rippling waves of pleasure. She allowed the tingling to spread throughout her body, and her pelvic muscles contracted briefly with a series of small jerks, as tiny sparks of light hit with precision between her legs. Daimon giggled with mischievous delight.

"My God! Help!" a female voice shrieked and echoed through the ward, and then, "Staff! Staff! Come quick!" Sari watched as a small troop of rubbery rickety robots rambled down the hall to the source of the noise. She heard a loud thud followed by a series of muffled cries.

Sari continued to work on her drawing, filling in the tiny stars and eyes that were swirling out of the divine yoni, ignoring, barely even hearing, the wild commotion about her. The moving image of a limp man being carried by four others reflected off the corner of her retina. The sound of a seclusion chamber door slamming reverberated eerily down Sari's auditory nerves, and mocking laughter continued to echo through the twisting corridors of her mind.

After completing her drawing, and feeling quite proud of it, Sari got up and began the journey down the long hallway to her room. Skipping down the hall she stopped in front of a large glass window and admired the wavering fun-house reflection of herself in it. She laughed and raised her leg up into a graceful ballerina stance, before skipping back down the hallway.

Ghosts and voices filled the corridor, which seemed to hold the echoing morphic memories of countless souls who had suffered within its walls. Wisps of madness filled the air. Sari noticed a cluster of shiny golden objects twinkling on the hall floor and stopped to curiously examine them. After recognizing what they were, she quickly bent down, scooped them up, and hid them inside her gown, amongst the tangle of hair sprouting from under her left arm.

Upon entering her bedroom, Sari noticed that her completely paranoid and totally perverted roommate was for once asleep. Thank God, she thought to herself, as her roommate snored. She's just plain fucking crazy, Sari mumbled to herself, flopping down onto her bed, staring upwards at the self-rearranging, three-dimensionally re-organizing, cream-sculptured ceiling, which dripped huge globs of warm ectoplasm onto her skin.

Sari watched as slippery, squirming snakes slid passion-ately into the love orifices of translucent crystal water babies. Daimon curled up cozily in Sari's overly-medicated brain, as she began to rub her fingers between her legs. Daimon simulated the sensations of a lover kissing and thrusting inside her as Sari masturbated herself to climax. Satisfied and sleepy, they dissociatively drifted off into a dream-filled astral excursion together.

Sari abruptly awoke several hours later with a start, when a pointed object jabbed sharply at one of her breasts. It was close to midnight, and the staff was changing shifts. She got up in slow motion, fluidly walked out into the dark empty dayroom like a silent specter, and peered into the brightly illuminated nurse's station, where several of the demonoid impostors were clustered together talking — about her she figured, because Sari knew that they always talked about her.

She looked down the long western corridor. All was quiet. She walked down the corridor, rolling her fingers along the wall, to it's end. She stood motionless with her face plastered against the window, and her hands up against the locked metal door, as she peered outward through the parking lot, watching moths dance in dizzy circles about the street lamps. She was smiling and giggling softly.

Turning around slowly and seeing a dark empty hallway, she reached deep inside her gown and quietly withdrew the bundle of keys that were snugly nestled within her armpit. The sweet smell of her own sweat and pheromones filled the air. She nervously tried to fit one of the keys, then another, and another into the slot to no avail.

A barrage of bangs on the door of a seclusion room down the hall a few feet from her sent a jolt of adrenaline into Sari's blood. She froze for an eternal instant, feeling her heart racing rapidly, sweat dribbling down her sides, then she quickly tried another key, and it slid right in.

"Sari," one of the demonoid puppets said, as he traveled briskly up the hall toward her, "you shouldn't be down here. Why don't you come back to the nurse's station and get a sleeping pill."

"Go Sari. Go now," her alien friend whispered through her. Quickly she turned the key and pushed the door wide open. A cool wind blew freedom against her face, and the moon blazed salvation brightly in the sky.

"Hey!" the mechanical male voice filled the air, "come back here." But Sari was gone, dashing now at top speed through the parking lot like an Olympian track star, running as fast and laughing as hard as she possibly could. She heard a crowd of shouts and footsteps behind her as she ran and ran, across the highway, into the woods, dissolving into the dark tangle of trees. She remembered now, as she ran, why it was that she was here, and what it was that she had to do. It all seemed so very simple.

CHAPTER I

I was in the shower, massaging a bad hangover under the hot water, when the earthquake struck. It's funny how I always seem to hear earthquakes before I feel them. Must be something to do with the fact that sound waves travel faster than shockwaves, I figured. Sometimes it seems that I'm even able to sense a forthcoming earthquake a few seconds before I hear it coming, as though there were some kind of electrical disturbance in the air around me.

The rumbling came — like everything always does — in waves, and I felt like I was on a tiny row boat out on a wild raging sea. I grasped the shower curtain for support, as the vibrations grew in intensity, each wave hitting a bit harder than the last. Everything was frantically shaking back and forth, and it crossed my mind, with an ominous soundtrack, that the ceiling might cave in on me at any moment.

The stream of shower water sputtered, and then suddenly stopped. The walls spun around me, and I slipped to the ground with a hard thud, pulling the shower curtain on top of me. After about forty seconds the tremors began to subside, the ground stabilized, and the shaking stopped. My dizzy head was pounding, stars flickered before my eyes, and my stomach felt twisted into knots. But, oddly, I felt hungry in some indefinable way. I sat there for a few moments, watching a tangle of glow worms tunnel themselves rapidly through my visual field, before I got up out of the shower and patted myself dry.

My place was a data-rich study in the messy mathematics of experimental chaos. Just about everything that could possibly have fallen did. Paintings had come off the walls. Bookcases and shelves had tumbled onto the floor, creating mountains of books and tangled electronic equipment, burying the hills of dirty laundry already there.

A few pieces of my ceiling had crumbled onto the floor, and several cracks ran jaggedly down the walls, but the basic structure appeared to have survived all right. I walked into the kitchen and grabbed a piece of cold solidified pizza sitting on the counter from the night before, and brushed off the broken pieces of plaster from the ceiling that had fallen onto it.

I sat on the floor, with my legs spread, and back up against the wall. I watched as rays of sunlight flickered rainbows through the window, and ate the chewy slice of pizza in deep thought. Clouds moved slowly across the sky of my mind. There were several major aftershocks which, strangely, seemed to punctuate the thoughts I was thinking at the time that they occurred. I love the way that earthquakes sometimes do that, and the way that they seem to just lift me right out of the mundane and into the moment. They give me this sense that I'm in the center of an immensely important drama.

I was in a state of terrible confusion. I felt like a piece of chewed gum devoid of any remaining flavor. I was amnesiac with regard to much of my past, and nothing made much sense to me.

What am I doing with my life? I thought in frustration, and the ground rumbled in response. Why does everything seem so damn difficult? The dresser shook, tipping my beloved Christmas snow globe off and onto the floor where it shattered. I guess you could say that things had not exactly been going well lately. My girlfriend had just left me, I had recently been thrown out of school, and I was suffering from fairly acute survival anxiety — the fear of being hungry and homeless, lost and loveless.

As the earth below me trembled, in my mind's eye I saw volcanoes spewing lava and giant landslides. It seemed as though the whole universe was going to collapse, and the weight of the entire cosmos was going to cave in on me. I felt ill equipped to deal with the world I was in, as though I was a small frightened child wandering around lost in a forest fire.

I found myself falling, spiraling downward. I had little will to carry on with life. The state of the planet that I inhabited didn't look much better than my personal situation. Things looked pretty grim all around, and my chances of getting out of this mess appeared to be as fruitless as searching for lost diamonds in the snow.

I thought that I heard someone say my name. "Nicholas," the soft voice whispered, and I could have sworn that I saw, however fleeting, the face of a beautiful dark-eyed woman in my mind's eye. She spoke to me in riddles and rhymes, "I am your long-lost sweetheart and best buddy personified, the one for whom you have always secretly cried." I stood up and walked over to the small closet under the staircase where the voice seemed to be coming from. I opened the closet door swiftly, smelling mischief in the air, and saw that there was no one there.

Then I heard what sounded like a small child giggling behind me. I turned around to see only my own shadow, pulsing and throbbing to my heartbeat. I walked over to the window and looked out at the Topanga mountains. The windowpane was spotted with tiny purple microdots. I wiped it clean to see out more clearly.

Great, I thought, now in addition to losing my girlfriend and my career, I was losing my mind as well. Well, my mind may be going, I thought, but at least I still have my sense of humor. I wondered if the phone lines were working. Just then the phone rang.

"Hello," I said picking up the receiver.

"Hey, how's it shakin'?" the familiar, sultry female voice inquired.

"That's an extremely complicated question Sari. I'm a little wobbly, I guess," Kato answered, realizing that he hadn't heard from the brat princess in over four months. "How's it waving your way?" he asked.

"Get this. I escaped from the psychiatric hospital last night, and now I'm on a mission to save the world. It's a dirty job, but somebody's got to do it. And that's just the tip of the ice cream cone! So hey, I'm here in the City of Lost Angels, just in time for the big quake. I'm not far from Topanga. Care for some angelic assistance?" she asked seductively.

My head was reeling. No, not Sari. Not now, I pleaded. I wanted to spend the day putting my place back in order, figuring my life out, and working on my unauthorized autobiography. Sari always meant more chaos.

"Sure, sounds great," Kato said without hesitation, unable to turn her offer down. We both realized the perfectly timed synchronicity of an earthquake striking the day Sari hits town.

Sari appeared to be graced by a kind of supernatural charm; angelic protection seemed to surround her. She walked confidently through the busy broken streets of Santa Monica, gracefully seductive, hands in her velvet-lined pockets, black hair spraying in the wind, secretly smiling, her piercing ebony eyes now bright and sparkling with rainbow refracted sunlight. A dazzling sight to behold. She appeared to meet the gaze of all who crossed her path, yet also seemed to hardly take notice of her surreal surroundings.

Lights were flashing everywhere. People appeared stunned, and some were bleeding or injured. A cloud of white dust from the crumbled buildings hung in the air, and here comes Sari, strolling through it all with the nobility of a princess. Feeling so full of wonderful crystalline visions, she was, and just brimming over like a brightly colored phantasmagorical fountain of dreams. It seemed as though the visions were a warm liquid substance swirling about within her.

Sari smiled each time she remembered what Daimon had told her — that all it would take was a simple kiss, or a devilish flick of her tongue, and then anyone she wished would also be full of the fluid visions. Daimon informed her that the extraterrestrial virus which lived within her was in actuality a nanotechnologically-engineered, self-replicating alien artifact from a faraway star system, sent across the galaxy as a catalyst to stimulate human evolution. Mesmerizing fractal forms danced like stardust inside her head, squirming, splitting, and reforming.

So full of vision she was! All it would take was one little kiss, and the vision stream would pour out of her, and into the neural pathways of any one she wished, continuing on its own course within them, just as it now flowed through her. Then they too would have the amazing power...and the awesome responsibility that came with it. The words from an old Rolling Stones song echoed in her bouncing head as she strolled up the 3rd Street Promenade, "Its just a kiss away... kiss away... kiss away."

I lay down on my bed, pulling a pillow over my head, and sank down into the ground. I found myself lost in a labyrinth of subterranean caverns deep below the surface of the earth. I walked about in total darkness, stumbling over rocks, feeling my way along the wall, bumping my head into stalactites hanging from the ceiling of the cave.

The glowing eyeballs of evil elves darted about, watching me from all directions. Slimy fanged creatures snapped frantically and bit at my legs. I heard the steps of someone walking behind me. I turned around and saw that it was Willard, an old childhood friend, who none of the other kids liked. Looking into Willard's sad eyes I felt as though I was on the verge of discovering some Great Secret, something of utmost importance that had always eluded me, yet was right under my nose all the time, when a knock at the door brought me quickly to the planet's surface.

I stumbled out of bed, yanked on a pair of tie-dyed tights, walked over to the door, and opened it. There stood Sari, sure enough, swaying back and forth, her hands tucked neatly into the front pockets of her faded, spray-on blue jeans, with a sly smile pasted on her face. Her eyes looked unusually bright and sparkling.

She was wearing a silver-studded, blue denim jacket, lined with purple velvet, out of which popped a white t-shirt, bursting with breasts. A silver chain dangled around her slender waist, and fell over her perky round bubble-butt. Her mouth was slowly engaged in the process of chewing gum, and she popped a pink bubble sharply between her glistening lips. She looked incredibly pretty, and seemed to twinkle with effervescent fizz.

"Hi sweetie," she sang cheerfully. They stood eye to eye. Kato bent forward to kiss her sweet pouty lips, but she turned her head to the side. He pecked her lightly on the cheek, feeling slightly surprised and hurt that she had turned away, and not understanding why.

"Wow, Kato," she began excitedly, "Have you checked out the quake damage? Downtown LA is in pieces. Freeway overpasses collapsed. Everything is total pandemonium. All hail Eris — the great goddess of chaos." Her eyes appeared to be leaping out of their sockets, and silver-orange sparks were crackling around her head. Ripples of energy seemed to be expanding out of her.

Kato nodded in response, and then began examining the imperfections in his fingernails. Sari walked into the kitchen and picked up a slice of cold pizza from the counter.

"Gee, well aren't you the talkative one," she said sarcastically, looking at him, but there was still no response. She brushed the plaster bits off the pizza. "God Kato, what is wrong with you? Do you have a porcupine caught in your throat?" she asked, then popping a large bubble between her lips. She was crunching cold pizza on one side of her mouth, while chewing gum on the other.

"Ginger left me," he said, playing with his fingernails.

"Oh, Darn!" Sari said with her tongue in her cheek, and then smiled. She had a piece of dried tomato sauce on her upper lip that she wore as part of her charm, and was swinging a pink flexible translucent key chain around her finger. Kato actually almost laughed for a moment, and the room momentarily brightened.

Sari giggled. She crumpled her adorable face into her hands, and said, "What do you care that some silly girl doesn't appreciate you? Gosh, it wasn't like she was your soul-mate or anything like that. Personally, I gave up on that whole idea of a soul-mate after I met my third one," she said giggling, "but maybe you and I can be sole-mates," she said laughing, holding the sole of her left foot flush with his.

Kato didn't laugh. She put her arm around him, and ran her long fingers delicately through his hair. "What do you really want?" she asked.

"To find someone as hopelessly insecure as myself, so that we can become pathologically dependent on one another, and live happily ever after," Kato replied.

"But," I interjected, "I suspect that I may be going insane. I've started hearing voices, and it feels like I'm on the fast train to Squirrel City. My mind is a storm of raging emotions, and my insight generator is hyperactive. I suspect that sometimes my brain continues to generate insights, even when there aren't any real ones left to be had. I think that my nervous system has been inventing delusional revelations."

"Trust me, you are not insane," Sari replied calmly. "Take it from someone who recently escaped from a psychiatric hospital. You're just a little broken-hearted, that's all. It'll pass. Uncertainty is really the only thing that you can always count on. The trick, you see, is not just in learning to live with uncertainty, but to actually embrace it, and be inspired by it, so that you remain unattached to the outcome of events beyond your control."

"Uncertainty freaks most people out, so we usually try to avoid as much of it as we can. We try to make our lives as predictable as possible, to play it safe. The futility of this process is that it inevitably leads us to the natural chaos of our own death — the greatest uncertainty of all. I say, surrender to the unknown! The big secret is this: it is the essential mystery inherent in all things that is at the heart of what makes life so wonderful," she said, continuing to move closer, "You just never know for sure what's going to happen next, now do you? And isn't that the thrill of it all?"

Just at that moment there was another tremor — a rather powerful one — and Sari stopped talking and smiled, as if the aftershock served to drive her point home. Everything began to rattle and more plaster bits rained down upon us. This is the closest we ever get to snow in Southern California.

She rubbed her hard ruby nipples sensuously against his arm, as her right index finger circled through the bristly hairs on his chest, softly blowing on his neck like an exotic musical instrument, barely listening to the almost inaudible words of protest coming out of his mouth.

While I recognized that there may have been some wisdom in what she was saying, I felt like she wasn't really understanding me, and — in trying to cheer me up — was making light of my painful situation. I knew that the voices that I had been hearing were not symptoms of simply a "broken heart", but I didn't say anything. It is often said that some things are best left unsaid, and this was especially true with regard to me making a sustained effort to defend my insanity.

She continued, "Things aren't quite as bad as they appear. They never really are. The act of being a conscious entity in this universe is just not meant to be taken nearly as seriously as you make it out to be. The best reason that I can come up with as to why the universe exists, is simply for divine amusement. Actually, it all depends on how you look at things. Don't ever underestimate the power of your own mind, because the universe is all in your mind. Up here in the clouds, you see, its all just good theatre."

"Who the hell is up in the clouds? I'm down here in the rubble," Kato protested.

"Hey c'mon dude, lighten up," Sari replied, "Get vivid. Look around. Shhh. Listen. *Can you hear it?* The whole universe is alive. It pulsates and throbs like a huge sexual organ all around us. Can you feel it Kato? Can you feel the universe pulsing and throbbing all around and through you?"

"I hear the refrigerator humming," he said, and then mumbled something incoherently.

"Silly boy, life is a grand adventure," she said enthusiastically, "Its a mysterious miracle."

"Spare me," Kato pleaded, lost in the land of shadows.

"Just try to relax, enjoy the show, and don't take it all so damn seriously," she continued, "Remember that things are not always what they seem. The beautiful and terrible and wonderfully weird thing about life is that everything can always totally change in the flash of an instant — into something completely new and different. Everything is energy, and energy moves in waves. All is composed of vibrations, which come in waves, and go in waves."

"So what's your point?" Kato asked, not really paying much attention.

"To notice the simple things. To pay attention. Experience the mystery, and partake in the miracle that is forever here to stay. Watch the way that sunlight sparkles rainbows through dewdrop-covered leaves," she said, while gently stroking his head again, as though she were trying to comfort a small child, but he didn't respond. Sari smiled as her devilish idea quickly grew to fruition.

"Well, in any case, I've got a special present just for you," she said, turning his head to face hers. Sari slowly slid her pink tongue across her upper lip, trailing a glistening sheen of saliva along its path. "I want to fuck your brains out," she whispered, "This is a rare opportunity, you realize, to transcend your mortal existence."

Her laser-beam eyes met his, and she passionately kissed him full on the mouth. He surrendered to her super-gravitational, electromagnetic charms with about as much sincere resistance as a pot of melted butter might yield to an incoming arrow, even as a part of him screamed out that he was once again baring his chest to the devil's claw. He felt as vulnerable as a blood-filled jellyfish surrounded by a pool of hungry sharks.

As Kato's psychological barriers were quickly dismantled, their tongues delightfully intertwined like wet horny snakes. The rest of the universe dissolved, while they melted together, and made passionate love on the living room floor for several hours. Aftershocks from the quake rolled through them, lifting them up like an ocean wave, and gently letting them down, as though in a dream.

Several hours later, as Sari was leaving to drive up the coast, she handed Kato a folded note. "Read this after I'm gone," she said, and began fondling the bulge in his pants, so that he wouldn't be tempted into reading the note right away.

"Thank you," Kato said, trying to sound as sincere as he possibly could, "Thank you for everything." She had completely won us both over in the end, and Kato and I were jostling each other for control of the body.

Sari smiled that mysterious smile that was her trademark, which I knew spelled trouble. "Don't thank me yet," she said cryptically, "It hasn't even started."

"Look!" Sari suddenly said as a shooting star blazed a trail through the dark sky. "Make a wish," she said. They both fell quiet for a moment and stared up into the Milky

Way. I looked into the heavens and wished for Sari to be mine.

"When you look out into space at night," Kato asked, breaking the silence, "do you ever feel strangely home-sick?"

Sari giggled, turned her head, and for a second, I swear I saw two metallic antennas sticking up from behind her ears. She said something, which sounded to me like Martian gibberish, and then, "Yeah, it makes me nostalgic for the future."

They kissed passionately, rubbing their bodies together under the moonlight, generating a soft auric glow of their own from the squirmy friction.

"Let's dance," Sari suggested, humming a tune, and setting the beat. Their bodies began to slowly wiggle and undulate to the night's rhythm. Soon the whole cosmos became like music, everything began singing, and Sari and Kato danced together under the stars, like individual notes in a universal hit song.

It was a magic moment. Hand in hand, they swung each other around wildly in circles, as the world blurred together. After a few minutes Kato, breathless and dizzy, collapsed on to the ground, as the smeared world spun around him. He watched with intoxicated fascination as Sari continued her mad pagan movements, smiling and laughing ecstatically at the heavens, as her body bounced gracefully about. Man, this chick was wild. Her energy was just incredible, and her enthusiasm for life was infectious.

Sari's hair outshined the moonlight, and her eyes out-sparkled the stars. She bent down to kiss Kato one last time. She was giggling, in a frenzy of sorts, and unable to stop moving. Before he could say another word, she quickly hopped into her little white Mazda, started the engine, and blew him another kiss. Then her car dissolved into the foggy darkness.

CHAPTER 2

As Sari whizzed off into the dark night, the stars blurred by in long silvery streaks. She flipped on her portable tape recorder, and began reciting her moonlight memoirs into the cool night wind.

My name is Sari Feline, and, no doubt, most of you are already familiar with my many hit music videos, and numerous top-of-the-chart albums. Judging by the large volume of fan mail I receive these days, and the way my albums are being snatched off the record store shelves lately, I think it's fair to say that I've earned my place in the nighttime sky amongst the stars. *Yum!*, my first album, went gold in three weeks, and my latest album — *Bite the Forbidden Fruit* — has sold over six million copies worldwide, and is still going strong. People are just eating it up, seeds and all.

I was born to perform, and just love to be the center of attention. Ever since I've been a child, I've always loved to sing and dance, and shake my body around. It's usually hard for me to keep still, even when there's no music wiggling through the air. My arms and hips are almost always in motion. But then again, there are times when I can sit perfectly still in deep concentration, and not move a muscle for hours on end. But even then, I'm dancing away to the music of the spheres in my imagination. I have a very active mind, and tend to do things in the extreme, for sure.

33

Part of my compelling mystique, I think, stems from my exotically blended Japanese and French heritage. I embody the genetic juncture where east meets west, where the past joins with the future. I have long silky black hair, large sensuous dark eyes, and a very curvaceous body with big voluptuous breasts and a perky round butt. I'm extremely beautiful and very sexy. Heads always turn whenever I walk into a room, and I stand out in crowds like a peacock in full bloom amongst pigeons pecking for food.

I have a sweet melodic quality to my voice, which almost makes me sound like I'm singing when I speak. And when I sing, well, I've been compared to whole choirs of angels. My dark eyes are extremely hypnotic, and my gaze can cast spells. I can cause people to drop things just by looking at them. I have an almost supernatural kind of charisma, and most everyone who meets me loves me, men and women alike. I can also be quite a bitch, if you catch me on the wrong day, but even then, I'm always a lovable bitch. Even in the most extreme of circumstances, I never lose these qualities, or my cool.

I'm very independent, and don't like to be told what to do. I like to do things my own way. Always have, and always will. I have a very strong will, and an even stronger sex drive. I get horny a lot, and love doing it with both men and women. I simply can't ever seem to get enough, and don't understand the meaning of the word inhibition. Sometimes I can make love for days on end, and my ever-dripping screaming yoni still aches and aches to be filled. It seems like the more I get, the more I want. Every moment of interface — between my body and the universal life force — pulsates with incredible orgasmic potential, and, to me, the entire cosmos seems to be composed of flickering erotic particles and undulating love vibrations.

I'm also very syneasthetic; that is, all of my senses tend to run and mix together. For me, music becomes waves of moving color, feeling, texture, and taste. When I perform, I go into a kind of high-energy trance, and completely blend with the music. It's almost as though the music already exists in another realm. All I do is find it, and merge into it. I simply become the music, and then the rest is easy.

Every so often I go a little bit mad, but I guess we all do to some extent. Actually, I've been told that it's part of my charm. If my nervous system gets a little too excited the circuits can overload, and my mind has been known to come apart at the seams. All kinds of weird things can leap in and out of my head then.

Like sometimes I see these little elves running really quickly across the freeway while I'm driving. Or the sky will suddenly open up, and angels will look down on me from the heavens, showering me with love and miracles. Other times it'll be dozens of tiny devils poking me in the ass while I'm performing. Oh well, I guess it's all just a part of living. Everyone's got to deal with something. For me, it's just this funny thing about my brain chemistry that sometimes dissolves away the cohesion of my sanity.

The only really major bummer about it all is when they lock me away in one of those damn psychiatric hospitals. That can be a major drag. But while I'm there it gives me a chance to work on my art, and I leave my body often to go time-traveling. I spend time wandering through the Library of Alexandria, dancing with primitive tribal peoples, and conversing with great historical figures like Van Gogh and Aristotle. And I travel to the far future, where I operate a body that conforms itself to my imagination, on a giant biospheric colony many times larger than earth, constructed techno-organically in deep space.

But, in regards to my sanity, I must admit that going crazy certainly has its advantages. It's partially the reason I'm such an incredible genius. Brilliance of mind stems from the rhythmic flow between breaking down and reorganizing one's mental world view, the flip-flopping, fluidly flowing dance between wild out-of-control chaos, and harmonious symmetrical order. I love to dance with the Mystery of Existence, to take her in my arms and kiss her deeply. To drink from her breasts. To rhythmically move back and forth between mindless confusion and cosmic order. Sometimes nothing I'm doing makes any sense to me, then everything shifts, and it all suddenly makes perfect sense again.

I'm here on this wayward misguided planet on a mission from God. Why else would a light-being of my stature and nobility come to such a backward world, where the natives still think that hair dryers, VCR's, and thermonuclear bombs are pretty neat ideas?

You see, I was sent to Earth by the head of Intergalactic Mission Control to help the low levels of consciousness on this planet evolve beyond disconnected ego bubbles into a true global intelligence. Once this is accomplished, Earth will be capable of conversing with the established community of ancient planetary minds that already inhabit the vast expanse of intergalactic space. Until that day — Sari Feline here, reporting for duty, and at your service.

But, thank God, I don't have to do it all alone. I have an ingenious best friend from another world here to help me do it. His name is Daimon and he lives inside my head. He knows all kinds of things — things like you just wouldn't believe. See, he's been up and down this great big universe, gathering secrets about the origin of existence, the true

nature of reality, and how to live in a state of eternal pleasure — and he shares all this with me.

We entertain one another playfully for hours. We sing
and dance together in a bodiless realm of pure imagination,
where we can take any form that we desire. Aside from the
fact that we're madly in love with one another, he's come
to this planet in order to teach me how to help save our
suicidal world from the nearby clutches of global disaster,
and send it off ripping into ecstasy.

But even without me and Daimon working toward
ecstatic global union, I'd still be extremely optimistic about
the future evolution of humanity. That's because I'm from
the future. The future, you see — where everything comes
together — is my true home. I know that — with the excep-
tion of natural disasters — all of the problems that humans
face are entirely self-created.

The wisest among us have always known that reality
construction is a creative enterprise; that the world is not
composed of the stuff of stars, but rather, the stuff of mind.
Even the most advanced of the primates are slow learners,
Daimon tells me, but like all evolving beings, we'll get the
hang of it eventually. In the end, all present conflicts will
be resolved, and all polarities will come together just beau-
tifully. You'll see. Then we'll be ready for the next step in
God's great plan.

You know, earlier this evening I just couldn't resist
giving the most precious gift I have to offer to my dear
friend Kato, whom I've been totally digging these days.
Ever since I became infected with the alien virus from outer
space that expands the mind-matter matrix beyond all
known limits, I've just totally loved giving it to others
whom I think would benefit from the mutational process of
merging their mind with God. It's an amazing power to be

in possession of. Just think of what one little kiss can do. One little kiss could change your life forever, make you immortal, and reveal to you the truth behind all things.

Are you intrigued? Now, if I were to kiss you — and a kiss from me, I know you couldn't possibly resist — then you too would become one of us, a post-human, designer being on your way to the stars and beyond. Would you like that sweetie? Hmmm? Do you want a little kiss? I promise to be gentle, but there's no turning back once you've taken the leap. Mmmm...was that a yes? Would you like to taste my tongue swirling around in your mouth, and travel to new worlds beyond your wildest dreams? Come closer then. Close your eyes, and pucker up. Here it comes you silly.

CHAPTER 3

I closed the door and shuffled sleepily back into my bedroom, noticing that Sari's presence remained quite strong. I saw my shadow move along the wall as I walked, and began to think about the nature of human existence.

It occurred to me that people, for the most part, unconsciously scurry about, mechanically repeating their little busy behaviors like ants; from birth to death they elevate their sense of self-importance to dramatic proportions, and remain completely oblivious to the startling mystery of their own existence — which would stop them dead in their tracks, if only they would notice it staring them in the face.

I sequentially reviewed all my daily behaviors with an odd sort of detachment, and saw the archetypal cycles of motion repeated in endless variations, by countless other people in Southern California, around the globe, across the galaxy, as part of a huge fractal wave that was unraveling throughout the universe. It was at this point, when I clearly witnessed how the *cosmos emerges from chaos,* that I developed an awareness of the unusual nature of my thought process.

I put Sari's note on my desk, planning to read it in the morning, and switched off the light. On my way over to the bed I stepped on something that made a loud crunch, but could not be bothered to see what it was. I lay down on my bed, dreamily watching the full moon out my window.

My mind started to roam, and I got to thinking about a secret doorway that I used to enter in the back of my bedroom closet as a child. It suddenly occurred to me that I might be thinking too loud. I did not want to wake up my landlady, who was sleeping upstairs, so I tried to quiet down my thinking as best I could.

It seemed that I was starting to fall asleep and enter hypnogogia, when the moon started giggling. Without warning, I lifted my eyes, and was suddenly swallowed up by a huge vortex of pink energy twisting upwards into space. It felt as though I was breaking through a series of warm membranes, into a great ocean of clear white light, out of which swam a billion fantastic forms.

I watched with awed fascination as luminescent streamers eerily traveled, like subcellular messengers, between the interstellar network of pulsing stars and myself. It seemed as though I was but another star in space, radiating light, and at the same time a single cell in a super-organism, receiving genetic transmissions from some highly intelligent, universal inter-galactic core-mind. I remembered a gold star that an elementary school teacher had put on top of one of my papers as a child, and I saw it in my mind's eye.

Then I started to feel nauseous, and my body began sweating profusely. My head was dizzy, and my heart was racing rapidly. I looked at the clock. It read 12:45 am. I recognized with escalating distress that my personality was literally dissolving, and I struggled to remember who I was. My name is Nicholas Fingers, I reminded myself again and again, but the words meant nothing. As I anxiously attempted to remind myself of who I supposedly was, Fleischeresque clowns did pinwheeling somersault acrobatics across the heavens.

My heart was beating faster and my mind was speeding. I took several deep breaths and looked at the clock again. It now read 12:46 am. I switched on the lights and walked into the bathroom. I splashed some cold water on my face and looked in the mirror. My eyes — wide with pupil dilation — appeared to be on fire.

Many different faces looked back at me — male and female, old and young, familiar and strange, joyous and agonized — all seeming to melt and morph together, back into me, whenever I blinked my eyes, which alone remained unchanged in the reflection. Dozens of smaller faces erupted simultaneously out of my head, shoulders, and chest; grimacing, laughing, crying, talking, singing, screaming, and reciting poetry.

I shook my head desperately and my bulging eyes stretched out and splattered on the walls, before springing back into their sockets like a pair of overstretched Slinkys. I staggered back into my bedroom, which now wavered fluidly before my eyes, and I felt like I had crossed over into Toontown, or cosmic cartoon consciousness. The floor felt as though it were made of Jell-O, and it was hard to keep my balance as the planet spun beneath my feet. Everything seemed to be vibrating at super high speeds, and all solid substances had become like liquids, flowing into one another, immersing me in a van Gogh landscape.

Tiny cartoon elf characters scuttled quickly about my room, leaving a ghostly crisscrossing pattern of miniature wisps and vapor trails behind them. Other critters crackled as they sped through the air, bouncing and ricocheting off the walls like balls of Silly Putty. Three-dimensional woodgrain movies emerged out of the walls. There were eyes everywhere. Everything was alive and watching me. Jeez, I thought, this could really make someone paranoid. I stared into, and simultaneously saw out of, the eyes of all-existence.

A tiny fairy creature flew onto the very tip of my nose and looked up into my crossed eyes. "How can this be?" I stammered. She whispered her response in a sweet musical voice, "It's all done with smoke and mirrors." Then she winked, smiled, and waved her magic wand like Tinkerbell, mysteriously vanishing into a bursting shower of luminescent fairy dust.

My head became filled with a million voices, a colony of buzzing beings. There was a crowd of people in my brain it seemed. As the voices grew louder, and the room started to spin, I lay back down on my bed. "Wow, what a view," I said, as I closed my eyes, and looked out over what appeared to be the Martian equivalent of the Grand Canyon. Jeweled archways, filled with multi-hued luminescent gels, and organic fountains spraying liquid light, suddenly erupted in a rapidly unfolding manner before my eyes.

I saw a community of smiling moustached Mexican faces then poke their animated heads out of large phosphorescent sombreros, and large sea monsters frozen in aquamarine green gelatin. The Aztec deity Xochopilli raised his hands toward the stars, as fireworks burst in the sky around him. Brightly colored fractal patterns emerged geometrically from the center of my mind's eye in endless combinations, as gurgling sounds squirmed and bubbled electronically through my brain.

The blossoming, stream-lined, multi-sensory, technicolor visions that followed, appeared to be superbly designed by a busy troop of nanotechnological Disney-elves. It seemed that these hyper-complex, micro-precisely crafted visions were woven together such that every image, every scene, every character, and every sensation that I experienced,

counted as a clue toward deciphering some ancient unfolding evolutionary riddle.

What ever happened to be happening at any given
moment, was always a perfect example of a higher lesson
that was being taught to me by some alien order of intelligence. I found myself shrinking down inside my own head.
What in God's name was happening to me?

Just then I heard a loud cracking sound coming from the
ceiling, and I looked upwards to see my roof being torn
away from the rest of the house. After the roof had been
ripped off, and the night wind rushed in, a giant white-
bearded face peered down at me with large loving eyes and
a compassionate smile.

I looked up into the illuminated face, which shone with a
light like none that I'd ever seen before. Although extremely bright, the light didn't hurt my eyes at all. I immediately
recognized this being to be a personification of God, our
living lord, and heard the sounds of heaven — angelic song
and mingled laughter — all around me.

I couldn't move, and just slowly opened my mouth up
and down, but no sound came forth. A riot of wild thoughts
raging within my mind condemned me to utter confusion
and complete paralysis. God reached down, and tenderly
picked up my shaking and trembling body. "You're being
reborn, my child. Surrender to the mystery," he said majestically with a sweet and reassuring voice. He held me close
to his face, then kissed the top of my head, and I felt a burst
of divine light permeate me to the core of my soul. He gently placed me back into bed and replaced my roof. I closed
my eyes, and it felt as though I were falling down, down. I
saw a vision of God and the Devil locked in passionate
sexual embrace.

My eyes popped open to stop the sensation of falling, and searched the room frantically. I looked over onto my desk and saw the note which Sari had given me earlier. I reached over and grabbed it. My eyes tried to focus on the jumping words. It read:

Kato:

By the time you read this note the first stage of the transformation will already have begun. Don't panic. Trust me, everything's totally cool. It happened to me several months ago, when I first became infected, you might say, with the awesome extraterrestrial virus. The first phase only lasts a few hours. After the initial adjustment process, you'll be remolded into a state-of-the-art, inter-galactic designer being. It really can be quite fun, and it's very much the happening thing, so don't get all bent out of shape about it. I hope that you're enjoying yourself. Further instructions will follow soon.

XX, Sari

Kato couldn't make much sense out of the dancing words. He looked down at the clock again. It now read 12:47 am. Everything in his brain was accelerating faster and faster, but time seemed to be oozing by slower and slower. He struggled to comprehend what was happening to him, to maintain some sense of identity, but, he soon realized, this was a losing battle.

The now expanding, dis-identifying pool of dissolving consciousness that leaked out of Kato's head soon began to ubiquitously fill the room, the planet, the galaxy, then the entire universe. Mechanically, his body responded to a faraway transmission, instructing it to pick up the phone and call for help, but the phone just melted into his hands like a hot gooey Gummy Bear.

CHAPTER 4

I awoke the following morning bathing in rainbows, surprised to find myself feeling considerably better. Sunlight splashed bright golden puddles lavishly onto the floor, and tiny sparkling dust particles swam lazily through the bright photon spears like Sea Monkeys. A sense of mystery tingled in the air.

I raised my head with a bit of effort, and looked out the window to see if the world had changed any during the long blurry night. The sky was green, the grass was blue, the birds were blooming, and the flowers were singing. Everything appeared normal, but my senses felt unusually cleansed, as though layers of consolidated grease had been removed, and my interface with the world of sensory stimuli seemed remarkably fresh.

In fact, all that I saw seemed to sparkle, to glitter with a rich inner glow, as if composed of microscopic jewels. I looked onto my carpet and saw with disappointment that the loud crunch from the previous night had been my glasses. But the amazing thing, I suddenly noticed, was that my vision was better this morning than it ever had been with my glasses on. Incredibly, I was able to see with a greater degree of sharpness and vividness than I ever had in my whole life. I had completely forgotten about the avalanche of insurmountable problems that had buried me up past my eyes the day before.

My attention involuntarily gravitated toward the telephone by the bed. A moment later the phone rang, and I slowly picked up the receiver with a strange sense of curiosity. The plastic phone felt warm, rubbery, extra-large, and unusually pliable on my face, as though it were made of Playdough.

"Boo! Hi Kato. How's my sweetie pie?" Sari's soft giggling voice spilled through the phone lines.

Kato looked at the Daliesque digital clock through a purple haze. The numbers wavered a bit, although he was capable of correctly deciphering the time as 8:46 am.

"Sari?" Kato questioned groggily in response, "Well, if it isn't the princess with hallucinogenic lips. I must confess, you certainly pack a powerful kiss my dear. Needless to say, I had quite an unusual night after you left. It felt as though I fell through a crack in the space-time continuum, into a series of parallel universes. But I think I emerged back all right. At least I seem to be in one piece, and I'm feeling a bit more solid this morning. I woke up convinced that today doesn't even exist."

"Cool," Sari replied slowly, chewing a wad of gum as she talked.

"So, what's up over in your corner of the universe?" he inquired, smelling Sari's cherry chewing gum through the phone, still quite sleepy and dazed from the long strange night. He rubbed the stars out of his eyes, and watched them float in circles around his head.

"I've been driving all night, soaking up the moonlight, singing to the stars. I drove across the Bay Bridge into San Francisco about an hour ago. I'm up here to check out the music scene. There's a renaissance going on here. I think I'm going to join a band," Sari said.

"I got real horny driving up here last night," Sari said after a moment's silence, letting the words linger in Kato's ears before she continued, "I had to pull into a rest area at 3:00 in the morning, where I masturbated myself in the car. I came twice thinking about doing you."

"Anyway," Sari continued, "once I relieved the tension between my legs, and was back on the road again, I got to wondering about a lot of things. Long drives can really send the wheels in my head spinning. I realized, as Los Angeles dissolved behind me, and the musky smell of my own pussy filled the air, that I barely even know myself. I felt like I was just a one-dimensional character in someone else's script, as though all of my existence was ultimately just an idea in someone's imagination. I can hardly remember any of my childhood. I don't even believe that the people who call themselves my mother and father are really my parents. How about you? What type of childhood did you have?"

"I was conceived in a private research facility, on a small island off the coast of south-east Africa, as part of a secret genetic experiment," Kato responded. "My mother was a direct genetic descendent of Jesus and Mary Magdalene, and although she was just an unborn embryo, the gametes are fully formed even at that stage. Her egg was fertilized in a hybrid solution of genetically-engineered spermatozoa constructed from the DNA of men carefully selected for their intelligence, ingenuity, strength, and beauty."

"Several months after my birth, I was sent to north-west Wyoming, where I was raised by a pack of wild wolves for several years. At the age of four I was kidnapped by a satanic cult that glorified human sacrifice, and traced its lineage back hundreds of years. They kept me locked up in a small cage, fed me human flesh and body parts, and only let me out when they needed me for their power-raising rituals. I escaped at the age of seventeen, and then spent many years walking the earth searching for my lost soul," Willard added, looking forlorn. Then Willard got up out of the body, and floated over to the window like a ghost.

"Very cute Kato. I guess that explains a lot. I realize you've got a mystique to maintain, and I think you actually enjoy being a enigma. It's part of your intrigue. I was raised by poodles and Yeti space aliens myself. Speaking of enigmas, are you familiar with MPD?" she asked from out of the blue. The colors in the room seemed to shift hue just ever so slightly.

"Sure, Multiple Personality Disorder," I said, remembering what I had read on the subject, "It's an extreme form of dissociation caused by severe trauma during the formative years of childhood. Distinct, independently functioning, personalities are created by the brain to deal with experiences of overwhelming pain and confusion. Once created, each personality then continues to exist as a separate entity. Often each personality is not even aware of the fact that they all share the same body."

Sari felt a mild electric current travel up her spine, and said, "I've heard that patients with MPD, like people who think that they were abducted by space aliens, usually complain about large gaps of time that they can't account for."

"That's commonly how they discover their condition, as usually only one personality can be in control of the body at a time. Although, strangely, many people who suffer from MPD don't know that they're multiple until they're in their twenties. It's only recently that the medical profession has accepted the fact that multiple personalities even exist. For years psychiatrists cast them into the same category as Big Foot and the Loch Ness monster," I continued.

"And what category might they go under?" Sari asked, as poltergeists stirred about.

"What I mean to say is they pose a big mystery. The uniqueness of each personality is extraordinary and uncanny. Consider this; there are personalities of both sexes, all ages and archetypal characteristics, and each has its own repertoire of facial expressions, voice pattern, handwriting style, talents, allergies, memories, and brainwave patterns. They even have their own dreams each night. I've always thought that each personality is actually an isolated cluster of neurons, a submodule in the brain, a mini-brain," I explained.

"Spirit colonies seem just as likely an explanation as neuron clusters," Daimon interjected through Sari.

"Whatever they are, we know that intense overwhelming pain or fear can cause consciousness to dissociate from the body, to split, so that only one fragmented portion of their physically-bounded being is designated to experience the overwhelming negative sensations. People can develop dozens, or even hundreds of these different personalities through repeated trauma," I continued.

"Okay, so that helps to clarify things a bit. Like most forms of mental illness," Sari said thoughtfully, "the disorder is illuminating because it exaggerates a condition that is present in all of us. God knows that I've got a multitude of people living inside of my body. Things can get pretty unruly in here sometimes, but a unifying self usually emerges, and my many selves usually become orchestrated into more order than disorder."

"You know," I added, "its funny that you should mention this subject, especially upon awakening. It reminds me of something vague, yet important, something I just can't quite put my finger on." I reached over to take a sip of water from the glass by my bed.

"Well," Sari said, "I bring this up because as I was driving up here I started thinking that planet earth is suffering from Multiple Personality Disorder."

"I can see the tabloid headlines now: Mental Illness Strikes in the Global Brain — Gaia in Search of Psychotherapy," Kato said laughing for the first time in a long while, spewing water out of his nose and all over himself. "What kind of childhood trauma do you think caused it?" Kato asked, as he tried to soak up the water with a towel by the bed. He could smell Sari's scent rising up from the towel.

"Satanic ritual abuse inflicted by evil space gods," Sari replied.

"The horny hermaphrodite vampire aliens from Dimension X," Kato responded.

"Kato," Sari asked in a more serious tone after the laughter died down, "Do you know who someone by the name of Nicholas Fingers is?"

"Nicholas? Why he's an old friend, a writer. He's a difficult character to pigeonhole. Either he's a kook or a genius, no one knows for sure. Maybe he's a little of both," Kato replied, as I listened inside, wondering how she knew my name. Sari was on to something. Her question shook Kato's confidence, although he did his best not to let it show. He felt like a four-legged animal that just lost one of its legs, and was attempting to balance itself by readjusting the remaining three.

"Actually there's more than one Nicholas," Willard said with an ominous tone to his voice, "the original Nicholas mysteriously vanished a long time ago."

"Hey, thanks for the valuable information sweetie pie," Sari replied suddenly, "listen I gotta run. I'm standing outside at a pay phone, it's getting cold, and someone's waiting to use the phone. I'm going to go warm up, and then crash. I'll call you soon. Watch for the starburst bouquet that I'm sending your way. Ciao for now. Kiss kiss."

"Wait, Sari, you've got to tell me more about this virus," Kato said, but the line went click, as I laid there puzzling over much of the phone call. So much struggle in life, all for just one brief splash in the sunlight, I thought to myself.

CHAPTER 5

I sat up in my bed and quietly contemplated the conversation with Sari, staring at a small black spider slowly crawling across the wall, when I began to feel a bit strange again. Willard was back in control of the body, and I heard a knock, knock, knocking on Satan's door.

I recalled vivid memories of classmates teasing him as a child, calling him Weird Willy, because he collected dead animals and made strange things with them. At the age of nine he dissected a living cat on my bedroom floor with a pair of scissors and tweezers. Then he reconstructed it according to his own bizarre anatomical geometry, mixing it with body parts from frogs, birds, and lizards. My mom came in the room screaming. The creature was actually alive.

I remembered how all the other kids, and even my dad, had ridiculed Willard because of his unusual experiments. He tried to bring a golem — that he constructed from plastic body parts, aquarium tubing, and animal bones — to life. He used to work on time machines, space ships, and matter transporters in his garage.

I recalled how he had a taste for drinking human blood, as he used to lick it off other kid's wounds. I began to see erotically-charged flashes of something, something which can only be described as unspeakable horror. I started to lose control, and felt as though I was standing right on the edge of a precipice.

His heart began pounding loudly in his chest, blood was soon throbbing in his brain, and yes, he was feeling very odd indeed. Suddenly bat-like creatures were banging their wings against the windows of his room, smearing and distorting their grotesque faces against the glass. Then the room began to change. The walls became metallic, grey and featureless, and the room shrank, transforming the space into a dark windowless prison cell.

"Welcome once again to the Dark Tower of Chapel Perilous, my boy," a voice spoke through the ventilation system to him, slightly chuckling, "We knew you'd be back. We kept your room for you just as you left it." He felt short of breath, sweat was dribbling off his forehead, and I grabbed hold tight of the Golden Bough. Willard stared the Devil in the eyes, and the Devil stared right back.

Willard could feel worms burrowing through his brain, devouring his mind. Overcome with sudden emotion, Willard began to cry, slowly at first, then gasping for air through his sobs. With tears streaming down his face, he reviewed with shame the necrophilic indulgences of his life.

Horrified by himself, by his uncontrollable passion for the dead, he looked at his fingers and saw a swarming mass of slithering squirming snakes that snapped up at his face. They metamorphosed into pulsating purple penises, that sprayed him with sickly sour semen. His worm-infested brain became inflamed, and began to enlarge, breaking through his skull, and burning with a bright blue fire. The floor suddenly cracked opened, and flashing flames leaped into the cell, licking and scorching Willard's face, which melted off and dripped into a black shiny puddle on the floor.

The black puddle grew into a gaping hole in the dungeon floor, that Willard somehow understood lead down to the darkest depths of the underworld. From this subterranean opening there gradually emerged a teeming troop of slimy zombies. Dozens of rotting corpses with faces that Willard recognized from the mortuary where he worked had sprung to life. All the "victims" of his pathological history now edged slowly toward him. The eerie moans and crackling cries of their excruciating suffering, and the smell of their decomposing flesh, filled the room.

Willard tried to scream, but no sound emerged from his mouth. His face was frozen in motion, as though he was in a horrible nightmare, The lustful living dead grabbed hungrily at Willard, tearing off his clothes, and lifted him into the air triumphantly. He struggled wildly in vein, as they carried him down down down into the dark hole in the floor. Roasting half-dead bodies, dangling from the ceiling on large metal hooks, brushed slowly against what was left of Willard's face, as he was carried down further into the dark foul-smelling pit.

Willard was suddenly thrown into what appeared to be an empty elevator shaft, still unable to scream as he fell, although he continued to try. He saw a beautiful woman among the zombies that were reaching out to grab him as he fell. He reached out and took hold of the beautiful woman's arm, which abruptly stopped his fall. There he was dangling in the elevator shaft, looking up into the large green hypnotic eyes of the woman's pretty face, when her arm suddenly ripped loose from its socket. Her laughter echoed as Willard tumbled down the empty dark elevator shaft with her writhing arm still grasping his hand.

Willard landed with a hard pounding schlop in a churning pit of snakes and boiling excrement. He managed to pull himself out of the smoking crater, stand up, and soon found himself running frantically through a complex twisting labyrinth, with more mad zombies slowly chasing after him from behind. He stopped to catch his breath, and peered into a well-lit chamber.

There he saw a long, dark-haired woman even more beautiful than the last, lying nude on her stomach, her buttocks raised slightly in the air, atop a large red satin bed surrounded by flames. She turned her head towards him and smiled, raising her eyebrows seductively, and pouting her large red lips into a slow-motion kiss. Unable to resist her supernatural magnetism, he walked toward her, and dove onto the bed. Willard kissed her impulsively, trembling to penetrate into the pink slit of creation. They began making love, and uncontrollably, Willard soon started to fantasize that she was dead.

He looked at her beautiful face and watched as she suddenly opened her mouth wide revealing two large twinkling fangs and a fiery forked tongue. Her eyes became a blazing bright neon red, that began to flash stroboscopically. The vampriss drove her razor-sharp claws into Willard's back, holding him steady and tight as she tore her mouth bloodily into his soft neck, like a praying mantis preparing to devour her lover. As she sucked the pulsing life juice from his neck, she began to grow, and soon she doubled, and then tripled in size. Two new arms sprouted out of her sides, and wings grew out of her back, as her body continued to expand.

She took the form of the Hindu Goddess Kali, complete with a necklace of human skulls around her neck, and lifted Willard up in the air by his hair, tearing out his heart with one of her claws. She pushed his heart into her mouth, chewing and sucking it, as blood squirted lavishly in all directions, dripping down her face and over her breasts.

Using all four arms to manipulate his body into the proper position, she tore off his genitalia in the next bite, swallowing it whole in a single gulp. Then she opened up her mouth, and stuck out her forked tongue to catch the spraying fountain of blood that came gushing out from between his legs. Just then more zombies flooded into the chamber.

It was Halloween in Hell, and dark spirits rose up in chorus to celebrate the anniversary of the demons' revolt against Satan. The zombies carried what was left of Willard off into a long narrow cave. His face had melted off, his neck and chest were torn open, his heart and penis were gone, yet he continued to live on in agony. He struggled in vain to break free from the body, but found that he was trapped in its corporeal mesh. His hands were nailed to a cross, and electrode probes were driven deep into the depths of his brain.

They sunk the cross into the ground, and raised him up into the air. His silhouette blended with row upon row of squirming victims impaled upon stakes and hung from crosses that stretched as far as the eye could see. Horrible moans, howls, wails, and screams echoed across the dark landscape.

Gathering around him with razor-sharp instruments, the zombies began to slice and peel back his skin and eyelids with surgical precision, exposing raw twitching bleeding pink muscles and eyeballs. The band of zombies about him then began painting a bitter stinging saltwater solution very delicately on to every exposed muscle with tiny brushes, under his armpits, up his rectum, behind his ears, in his eyes, and up his nose.

A large, grotesquely disfigured construction engineer with empty eye sockets drove a ear-piercing jackhammer drill screaming into the center of his chest with extraordinary technical precision, right where his heart used to beat, and turned on a high-frequency electric current in his brain that greatly amplified the painful cascade of sensations. Willard experienced a peak moment of horror when he felt Satan's jumbo-sized flaming penis being forced deep up his ass, tearing and roasting his rectal tissue, as the Devil's merry laughter filled the air, co-mingling with the smoke rising up from his behind.

Small winged demons fluttered about Willard like evil butterflies or vampire fairies, biting off mouthfuls of his flesh, as the Devil continued to fuck him up the ass with his bright red cock. The driving burning pain was pushing Willard to the limit of what his mind could handle before passing into unconsciousness.

As the Devil's cock burst through his intestines, spewing flaming gobs of satanic semen laced with hot acid, Willard's body began to dissolve. The ground below him yawned open once again, and the biomorphic mush that he had become slid off the cross and ran down the expanding hole, like water swirling down a sewer drain, into the sizzling spiritual fires of purification below.

Every last toxic droplet of Willard's screaming spirit essence was efficiently extracted out of his corporal remains, as the illuminated meat passed through a series of fine mesh filters, which separate spiritual juice from undesired material impurities. Willard's spirit was extracted, compressed, and propelled through a long series of decaying pipes and organic tubes which fed into a humungous pit of fire, the grand furnace which fuels the great rumbling engines of Hell.

Here, immersed in the mother of all flames, his soul was purified still further, as all of his poisonous obsessions and desires helped to fuel the fires. What did not burn, or rather, what remained was this grey oily kind of paste. Off it went, flowing down a long assembly line, where the spirit-plasma solidified into something vaguely reminiscent of gelatin. It was flattened and rolled into long grey translucent sheets, similar in consistency to what are popularly known as "fruit roll-ups", only not nearly as sweet to the taste.

After a series of mechanical "vrrrrrrs" and "ka-chunks", thousands of Willard miniatures were stamped out of the rolling spirit-batter, like gingerbread men cut from a sheet of cookie dough. Tiny Willards — each one a holographic compression of his being entire — rolled down the nefarious assembly line like toy soldiers. Mechanized demonoids wired together their miniature nervous systems and programmed the circuitry in their tiny brains, like automated robots building televisions in a Japanese electronics factory.

Out they rolled on their backs, several thousand little smiling Willards, purified of sin, cleansed of karmic residue, and liberated from earthly obsessions. Eyes blinking with infant wonder, the living dolls rolled into giant black ovens, where they were to bake for several hours, and complete the alchemical transformation before returning to the surface.

CHAPTER 6

With Willard's spirit purifying in the ovens of Hades, we began to feel lighter and crisper, yet still somehow off balance, as we needed time to readjust to the shifting dynamics. I dropped my car off at the garage early that morning, and was planning to spend the day just taking it easy, maybe getting some long put-off writing projects underway, and contemplating the weird series of bewildering events that I had been experiencing.

I casually opened my front door to let some high-noon sunlight sweep the living room clean of evil spirits. I curiously witnessed my landlady's lover Jim, dressed in his usual baggy pair of paint-stained overalls, dashing down the wooden stairs, frantically turning on all the water sprinklers. He darted about with the single-minded concentration of someone on an urgent mission. I looked up in surprise, raising my hand in an expression of greeting, attempting to ask him what all the hurrying was about, when he quickly inquired as to my plans for evacuation.

"Evacuation?" I questioned, thinking that he must be joking.

"The fire storm is coming down fast over that ridge, and if you want to be around to see tomorrow's sunrise you had better hurry your butt out of here," he told me, pointing upwards behind him. "Shouldn't be more than a hour before the blaze reaches the spot your standing on," he added, spitting a glob of some unknown material out of his throat and into the garden.

I looked up and saw giant clouds of puffy white smoke rising up over the ridge, forming these unusually beautiful multi-layered patterns. Once the visual information struck my retina, a double shot of adrenaline and corticosteroids squirted into my bloodstream, and my nervous system shifted in nanoseconds to hyper-alert.

Time began to slow down, and things started to move in ultra slow motion. Every biological concern collapsed into the extremely focused moment, and all of the little forest animals inside of me jumped into a state of bio-survival alert. Life took on incredible vividness. It became impossible to read reality as a Buddhist dream illusion. Suddenly everything became very real, and all the little things began to really matter.

"But my car is at the mechanic's being repaired," I protested, scanning the environment for more information.

"Well, you'd better do something pretty quick there young fellow, because you're about to become one more crispy hors d'oeuvre in the belly of the fire goddess," he said with a hearty laugh, and then disappeared around the back of the house, still laughing, to turn on more water sprinklers.

I ran over to the phone as fast as I could, and picked it up. The line was dead. I clicked the receiver up and down a dozen times or so with no luck. No, this just can't be happening, I thought, today was supposed to be the day that I was going to relax and readjust. I ran to my bedroom. My other line was dead as well. I ran up the, now slippery, wooden stairs, through the garden, to my landlady's quarters, only to find that her phone line was also dead. Smoke was heavy in the air, and growing thicker by the moment. It was several miles down the mountain to Topanga Canyon Boulevard, then still many more miles out of the canyon to the coast or valley.

"I don't have a car, and I can't reach my mechanic because all the phone lines are dead," I explained as clearly as I could between gasps of carbon-heavy air. "Can I ride with you?" I asked in desperation. Smoke was rapidly coming down the hill towards us. The whole ridge above us was completely ablaze, and our neighbor's horses were storming about wildly.

She agreed, reluctantly it seemed, to allow me to come. I guess she didn't exactly feel comfortable saying no under the circumstances. I mean, although I'm sure she always did consider me to be a bit strange, I don't think that she was ready to handle the karmic responsibility of my death on her conscience.

So back down the wet wooden steps I ran, sliding down hard on my butt several times. Back in my place I began to wildly search for what I was going to take. I ran around my apartment in a frenzy. "Oh my God! What should I take?" I repeated over and over, running around in circles like a headless chicken on amphetamines, slipping and falling on the floor again and again. Okay Nicholas, an inner voice reasonably advised, don't panic, just stay calm and try not to panic.

I just couldn't seem to get a grip on what was happening. I yanked my box of journals loose from under the loft, letting a stack of boxes tumble to the floor. My place was still in chaos from the earthquake several weeks back, and it was difficult to locate things. Gotta hurry, I thought, brushing aside Sari's clothes and Willard's bones.

Up the stairs I ran, through the garden sprinklers, with my precious box of journals, crammed with the results of many years of carefully-recorded metaphysical experiments, and secret mathematical formulas regarding the interaction between form and spirit. I deposited them in the driveway, and ran back down the stairs.

My photo albums, I thought, I must get my photo albums, and my rare hermaphrodite erotica. Into the house I ran, and then out again with an armful of photo albums. Up and down the stairs I ran, breathlessly, carrying boxes full of writings, half-started books and articles, irreplaceable traces of my life, as the smoke began to fill my lungs, and the scorching heat from the blaze began to make me dizzy and lightheaded.

My lungs constricted into an asthmatic panic and I collapsed to the ground. Unable to stand up, I just lied there, and for a brief moment I only wanted to succumb to the flames, to just surrender to the mountain of fire. It was at this moment that I drifted up and out of my body, above the house, above the mountains, and watched as rivers of fire ran through the Malibu mountains, reminding me of the way that volcanic lava flows through the mountains of Hawaii. I realized at this point that the wall of flame was alive; she was an intelligent entity that sought to be understood.

I began to dialogue with the fire goddess, who's purpose — she explained — was to spiritually purify the mountains, which were infested with dense beings obsessed with materialistic fetishes. She was angry, spewing forth her rage. "Anitya," she roared, "all that exists must know impermanence."

Indian spirits rose up inside the tremendous belly of the goddess, and I recalled a dream that I had had weeks before about literally burning up in strange kind of sexual ecstasy. I was frightened with regard to how good it felt in the dream, because I knew that as delightful as it seemed, in reality I was burning alive, and I now became afraid that my negative thoughts were somehow helping to fuel the fire. So I tried to think more positively.

The sexual urge to merge rose up inside me, and grew out of control like the roaring fire which consumed all in its path. That is, all but the spiritually purified essence. My mind swam in a sea of sexual images. All around me bodies slid in and out of each other, morphing and melding together. Gasps and moans, mmmms, ooohs, and aaahs rose and fell in echoing waves as my ego started to melt. A twisting orgy of shiny bodies and intertwined limbs twinkled with shiny, thick, slippery juices that mixed and mingled together. Tongues and genitals strained in insatiable hunger as shimmering bodies trembled amongst the flames. Droplets of love juice sizzled when they met the fire.

The Fire Goddess consumed it all. She briefly took the form of the Hawaiian deity Pele, then the Hindu muppet-faced lord of the universe Jagganatha, and then the great Celtic figure Sheela-na-gig. She appeared before me — an astral mix of fire and flesh — with a wide smile across her face, and her legs spread open wide. Without hesitation she pulled my astral face into her giant bushy pussy, gushing plasma between her legs, for a hot and sloppy get-acquainted kiss.

Then cupping the back of my head — now slippery with her thick vaginal fluids, and red-hot from the flames — she unabashedly ground her flaming cunt into my face, eventually nudging my entire head inside its fiery membranes. For a moment I started to panic, fearing heat and suffocation. But I quickly discovered that since I was in my astral form the heat seemed bearable, even exciting, and if I moved in the right rhythm, I could breath alternatively between the thrusting motions.

I felt her vaginal muscles contracting rhythmically around my head, as I rammed it in and out of her, the flaming pit of birth and death. The flames felt like liquids running over me now, as they shot out from all sides of her with each one of my thrusts. I had to close my eyes, and the taste, the smell, the squishy sounds, filled my senses and overwhelmed me.

I let my tongue hang out of my mouth. It rolled smoothly over her wet tangy flesh, which sweated warm love droplets, filling my mouth, nose, and ears with her delicious juices and jellies. It became hard to breath, I could barely catch my breath, and at times her smell became nauseating, but I was incapable of stopping.

I strained to push myself as deep inside her as I possibly could, like I was attempting to return to the womb, the source of all creation. I increased the speed and intensity of the thrusting, and my head began to feel like it was going to explode. Sheela grabbed my buttocks in a frenzy and pulled me in and out of her, like a human-sized penis plaything. I felt her pushing me in deeper still, into a sea of raging fire.

My shoulders started to move inside of her, as she gasped several octaves lower. In and out I went, a bit deeper each time it seemed. She was now submerging my arms and chest, and sometimes I went in as deeply as my waist. I was moaning in vibratory rhythms, moving faster and faster. Smoke curled up wispfully from my astral flesh, as ethereal flames began at last to consume my metaphysical form.

Deeper and deeper she sucked me in, banging my head repeatedly against her cervix. She wiggled her body convulsively, fiercely yanking me in and out of her. When the goddess came, her thunderous orgasm squeezed my burning head so tightly that it popped, like a fluid-spouting marine mammal, and a volcanic rush of flaming cerebral spinal fluid streaked with grey matter burst inside of her reproductive tract. The whole universe trembled and shook, as my astral brain exploded in orgasm, spewing out my insides.

The boundaries between myself and the external world vanished for several moments — the fire spirit raged inside my soul — and then in a flash I snapped back into my biological body. Fear gripped my body by the neck like a skeleton's hand. But as my will rose up with great strength within, every suicidal consideration that I had ever had my whole life suddenly vanished, and I knew with renewed motivation that I wanted to live! No question about it. I wanted life. I struggled to stand, realizing that the approaching clouds of smoke were gaining momentum.

I made it to the driveway with my five boxes, and collapsed again to catch my breath, when my landlady informed me that I had too much stuff, and I had to bring some of it back. Police cars circled the area, announcing from their bullhorns to evacuate. Helicopters flew overhead. Now everything took on a dream-like sense of unreality.

"You can only bring what you can fit on your lap," she told me. I watched as she filled her car trunk with piles of clothes, as I headed back down the stairs with my life's work to leave in my apartment as a potential sacrifice to the rapidly approaching fire goddess.

Coughing from the smoke, my body tingling from hyperventilation, I locked up my quarters, and ran, two steps at a time, back up the stairs. I could now see flames leaping over the ridge, as I packed myself into the passenger seat of her Mercedes. I was sitting in the seat next to my landlady, still trying to catch my breath, when the door next to me suddenly flies open and there's Jim standing there, looking real upset and nasty.

He tells me that he's sorry, but there is just no room in the car for me. Realizing that he's far more concerned about his beer rack than my existence, and too inspired to argue, I quickly leap out of the car, strap all my belongings onto my back, and start dashing toward the neighbor's yard. "Easy now sweetie," I said, trying to calm the wild-eyed horse as I attempted to straddle her. After a few tries, and after almost getting thrown off more than once, I managed to gain her trust. Together, we galloped down the mountain.

Flames danced on the ridge behind us. Police sirens swirled surrealistically through the haunted hills. Fire engines raced by, leaving a red blurry trail behind them. Like a monstrous dragon, the flames raged down the hillside, as we descended out of its fiery clutches, towards the relative safety of the main boulevard. The whole mountain side was now ablaze, and flames were leaping towards us, chasing us down the mountain.

I invoked a flock of guardian angels to protect my house, and I visualized huge waterfalls cascading down over its roof. I prayed. Under the circumstances it seemed to be all that one could do. I watched the spirits of the forest animals and plants rise up with the smoke from the hills, like the harp-playing angels that ascend from extinguished cartoon characters, as we galloped off into the sunset.

CHAPTER 7

I rode my neighbor's horse south down Pacific Coast Highway, galloping around the endless stream of bumper-to-bumper automobiles. Sari was up in San Francisco rehearsing with her new band, and I didn't have a clue as to how to reach her. Maybe she wanted it that way. Once I got to Santa Monica, I let myself down off the horse, and set her free on the beach. I walked the rest of the way to Sari's studio, not far from downtown Venice, where I knew a secret key was hidden under a rock by the front door.

I let myself inside, and deposited all of my worldly possessions onto her shaggy carpet with a loud thump. Her place was virtually barren, with only a large futon on the floor, some loose clothes tossed about, and an electric guitar in the corner. There was also this eerie illuminated globe, which hung on a carved wooden stand by the bathroom door, like a lone specter watching over me. I collapsed onto her futon with exhaustion, kicked off my tennis shoes, and tried to make some sense out of my completely shattered reality.

I was massaging my swollen brain with my both hands, consoling myself with the comforting thought that at least things couldn't possibly get any weirder than they already were, when suddenly I began to feel a bit woozy, and my equipoise began to wobble. I started to wonder if the planet was spinning too fast for me. I braced myself, and attempted to prepare, as best I could, for whatever strange encounter might be headed my way.

My head grew lighter, after which my whole body started humming and then went numb. Perceptions began to fuzz, and boundaries began to blur. Colors ran and smeared together. Sensations, thoughts, and feelings became fluidly flowing, like hot candle wax. Sounds became elongated and reverberatory.

There was a high frequency ringing in my ears, my whole head was buzzing, and I started to feel very confused about what was happening. I thought that I heard the voices and whispers of old friends and relatives talking to me, although I couldn't quite figure out what they were saying.

The floor of the studio suddenly started to slant sharply, and I began slowly sliding down the tilting futon, down a massive dark mountain, into the seething swamp where all life began. Human heads floated about like apples in a tub of water, bob bob bobbing in the slow waves. A massive pterodactyl rose up out of the swamp, spreading its primitive reptilian wings, as it transformed into a glittering angel.

I suddenly became overwhelmed with the fear of death, of non-existence, and my body trembled briefly with a high pitch of acute anxiety. But the fear soon melted, for it now seemed that to biologically die, to loose the ordered structure of information patterns that I had so carefully collected and organized throughout my existence, was rather like one tiny software program being erased from the memory of an inter-galactic computer system, that was as vast as the universe itself. I was designed to contribute to the whole what I could, and it was really no big deal if I was lost, it seemed, for what I had accumulated was but one small drop in a great sea.

Then I thought, well, somebody has got to be doing what it is that I do, so it might as well be me, and my unique contributions then took on a grandiose sense of cosmic importance. That is, I realized that I had a very unique and essential role to play in the scheme of things, and actually, no one else could possibly play that role but me. This universe needs me as much as I need it. So that's why I exist, I thought with satisfaction, as my perspective shifted from microbe to messiah.

I felt like I was sinking deeper and deeper underwater, into an warm oozy soup. Bubbles rose all around me, tickling my skin, as I continued going down... down... down... into the very ocean of my being. At some point in the descent I became conscious of the economic interactions being dealt between matter and spirit that manifest as what we call life. Time began to stretch, and within moments, I seemed to have become a subcellular entity, something like a twisted DNA coil.

Genetically aware of my unique function, I swam inside the nucleus of a large one-celled organism, which, in turn, floated inside an incredibly huge pond that filled the entire universe. The information pattern that I had previously defined as myself seemed rather insignificant once I was confronted with the vastness of this far grander universal information network all around me.

The fragile amoeboid membrane, separating that which was defined as "I" from all else that existed, began to bulge, tremble, and suddenly it burst wide open like a popping bubble. The universe rushed into me like great gushes of water, and I went pouring out into it. After this initial rush, a relative equilibrium was achieved, and I became the Great Quantum Tao, as it were. So this is death, I thought from a vantage point far far far out of my body, where one's previous existence takes on the form of long epic dream.

It was at once both frightening and fascinating to awaken from the dream of life, as well as unsurpassable joyous release. I tried to remember to "let go, and go with the flow," as Sari had once suggested. I recognized that death can actually be a huge sigh of relief, and that one should never be frightened of losing anything, including their body, because the core of one's self is indestructible, eternal, and stubbornly immortal.

I began to morph, again and again I fluidly changed form with ease, and soon my protean self emerged on a whole new plane of existence. I was filled with the marvelous sense of unexpected surprise that a cluster of feces must experience, after being gently squeezed down a warm rectal passageway, and suddenly being propelled out of the body, into a cold pool of water, which begins its journey into the inner sanctum of underground plumbing networks.

I found myself in a rather crowded inter-dimensional well-pool, that served as an intergalactic central depot, where brave inner-space travelers from all over the universe came to meet one another.

Here, one becomes a visual expression of whatever one imagines oneself to be, changing form at will. The astral architecture that we inhabited seemed to be woven together by the very consciousness of those present. It seemed that a party was in progress when I arrived, and everyone was celebrating and having a rather festive sort of time.

To avoid all the commotion, I discovered a hidden trap door in the soft membrane floor of the chamber. I opened it, and went bubbling through, finding many intricately branching pathways that lead into a series of crystalline chambers, each housing different types of fantasies or realities.

I felt myself morphing again, and now it seemed as though I was moving in a car along a high mountain cliff, in a long boat through an Italian canal, then in a pushcart train clickily descending down track into a dark underworld. I was squeezed through a long slippery biological tube lined with twisting tongues and wiggling breasts, into a bright bathing golden white light.

I became the spark that precedes all existence. I heard Tibetan monks chanting, and found myself in the catacombs of a Gothic mausoleum, lying on a pulsating tomb, among countless rows of slithering ancient crypts, that were filled with mysterious forbidden secrets about the nature of existence.

Bodies came and went like snowflakes dancing in the wind. Tumbling into a temporary state of relative stasis, I spotted a transcendental object spinning in space before me and grabbed hold of it. It shone brilliantly in my hand, like a miniature star, and seemed as though it was composed more of energy than physical form. Its shape changed and shifted through various dimensions of geometric arrangement before my eyes. I marveled at it's intricate complexity, and somehow seemed to understand that it represented a sacred technology from a highly advanced civilization. I closed my right hand tight around the mysterious object and held it close to my heart. Then my body dissolved again.

I found next that I had become a giant brain floating in outer space. Dangling from my countless nerve terminals were a complex tangle of intricate wires, each of which were connected to a piano-like keyboard. With astral hands I found that I could play the keyboard, and got several alternating harmonies and rhythms going at once. This allowed me to orchestrate a glittering rainbow of magical musical sensory sensations in my giant planetary brain, creating a cascading myriad of marvelous dancing reality fabrications.

My brain, now a flickering flurry of molecular activity, began tuning itself through a wide variation of oscillating frequency patterns, and I began to pick up psychic televisions and extraterrestrial commercials from all over the universe.

I saw squirming orgies of rapidly moving figures, then a row of mechanical turtles raising their butts into the air, as a never-ending stream of alternate realities began to appear. Universes that could be, or maybe were, flipped by, one after another, in rapid succession. Waveforms collapsed from the quantum sea of possibility into brief flickering actualities.

I curiously watched a huge grey Geigeresque landscape biomechanically undulate below me. Tiny busy elf workers were scuttling about very quickly in a multicolored yarn factory. Then I saw subterranean mariners tug a giant glistening vampire Madonna through murky underworld seas.

The scene dissolved into a pretty woman sucking on an erect penis, which transformed into a beautiful long stemmed flower that she was blissfully smelling in a luxurious garden. A horse drawn carriage — driven by a knight sitting beside a demonic gargoyle — moved ominously toward me in slow motion. The gargoyle metamorphosed into a Victorian angel as they came closer, which began to flutter and fly.

I found that I had now become just a single point of consciousness. I was simply a point of view, a ghostly hovering bubble of awareness, able to observe a cascading multitude of three-dimensional, alternative realities, under close inspection. That is, "reality" became like those connect-the-dots games we play as children, and a whole series of amazing alternating possibilities arose one after another.

It seemed that anything could happen, that I had stumbled upon the very machine language that programs the creation of reality itself. I found that, like with lucid dreaming, after a little practice I could devise any type of reality that I wished to inhabit. With the wild-eyed, gleeful exuberance of a child-god, I divinely created whole universes that would dissolve afterwards like ice melting in the sun.

Being unable to avoid the temptation, I retained the structure of my ever-inflating ego, and began resonating with the heroic archetype in my own personal mythology. I felt like I was a divinely-appointed frontier scout exploring the edge of a new species horizon, like the first fish on land, like the first man on the moon. I had journeyed to some alien territory where no human consciousness had ever ventured before. In order to leave the signature of my precious ego, I planted a flag in the soil of the communal imagination, with the cover of my first book on it, so that future visitors passing through this underground network of inner spaces would know that I — Nicholas Fingers — had been there.

Then it seemed as though I had entered a space where I could now plan for the future development of my own personal form, engineer my own karma, and design my own destiny, by revising and editing my mind's underlying programming. I was also able to distribute a sparkling shower of inspiring messages into the time-stream of my life, which would arrive downstream and brighten up future events, when they actually happened, even if I didn't remember my having done this, after this experience was over.

After a time, I began to develop, what can only be described as an emotionally-vacant, *hunger for form.* The reality that I had left behind was so distant that I couldn't see it with a telescope. My earthly existence seemed so very far away, like another lifetime. Soon I started to repetitively wake up, in a manner of speaking, through various dimly lit, spatially reorganized, alternative versions of Sari's studio. It seemed like I was shifting through a series of parallel universes, each one a minor variation of the last, until I finally arrived back in the original prototype.

At one point it seemed that Sari's studio was attached to the end of a long robotic arm connected to a huge orbiting spacecraft, and my physiology was being carefully monitored by a brilliant team of neuroscientists from the far future. I could feel them making all sorts of subtle structural adjustments in my brain with their post-terrestrial technology. My body and mind seemed only loosely held together, and would ever-so-easily drift apart.

I discovered that when I moved my eyes to the lower left, I would get a digital readout of all the neurotransmitter ratios in my brain, superimposed on that corner of my visual field. If I let my eyes defocus on my surroundings, my perception would shift. Entirely new multi-dimensional realities would emerge, like when one stares into the abstract chaos of a computer-generated, random dot stereogram, and a three dimensional image emerges from the two dimensional surface.

Plants sprouted and began growing all around. Long green vines climbed the walls, transforming the room into a mini dripping tropical rain forest. Bulging organic peppermint-striped tubes pumped a deep purple energy juice through a branching lattice of veins in the pulsing biomorphic chamber surrounding me. Cute cuddly cartoon critters from my childhood walked out of the walls, and soft blanket trains rose up out of the carpet. Little castles grew out of my bed and body. It sounded as though I was switching through a series of radio stations, as glittering Christmas toy scenes flickered in my mind's eye.

I lifted my arm into the air, and watched as dozens of exotic birds flew out of it. Bubbles floated all about the room, each one more complex than a Faberge Egg, containing a whole universe within it. The ceiling became transparent and I could see the stars twinkling in the sky above me.

Then, I suddenly wondered with curiosity, if anyone had ever masturbated while fantasizing about me, and if so, what scenarios they had imagined. I began to laugh thinking of the possibilities. Then I remembered that I had seen a giant prehistoric dragonfly as a small child, and how I sadly discovered that when I told others about it, no one ever believed me. I looked at my knees and they became enormous mountains with tiny little cars driving up their small spiraling roads.

As I watched the tiny cars circling my knees, once again, I felt on the verge of remembering that Great Secret, something very ancient and timeless, that I could never actually grasp, because it seemed to disappear the moment that I would fully turn my attention towards it. It appeared that there were just certain things that one simply can not know so long as they are embodied in biological form.

The experience began to fade, and started to become difficult to remember, like a dissolving dream. What were astonishing revelations just a few moments before, now seemed like half-coherent clichés. The more I tried to recapture it, the more it eluded me, like trying, in vain, to grasp onto running water with my fingers. I remembered digging my hand through a cereal box as a child, crunchily hunting for the hidden prize inside, and this scenario then became an enlightening metaphor for how I approached my life.

I thought of Sari. A warm sweet feeling of unconditional love washed over my spirit, and I silently thanked her for the precious gift. Everything seemed to be totally all right with the whole cosmos, and the entire universe seemed to be cuddling me like the pink inner walls of a mother's womb.

I felt like I was being remolded into a new type of designer creature, and with it came the realization that "I" was composed of many many beings. The realization struck us all in a single moment of multiple illumination. But, it was still so very complicated inside, for, you see, our many inner selves were composed of many multiple selves themselves. Selves within selves within selves.

We rubbed our forehead, and watched our finger tips through our newly opening third eye. Each one of our fingernails seemed to have a unique personality all its own. The membrane that previously separated us from each other, and the rest of the universe, was now more permeable, less rigid, and we no longer felt so separate from one another.

We also no longer felt, well, merely human, for lack of a better expression. The universe, we realized, is simply an elaborately designed puzzle with a punchline, that is solved when the correct sequence of contingencies are clicked into place. Maybe we weren't so crazy after all, we said to ourselves, as we wiped the wet brain out of our ears. I opened my right hand, and looked down at the shining transcendental object, still metamorphosing against my palm.

CHAPTER 8

Sari returned from San Francisco at around noon, and didn't seem too surprised to find me sleeping on her futon. She acted pretty casual about me being there, and seemed rather self-absorbed. She didn't inquire much about the fire storm, and began raving about the constellation of people she discovered in San Francisco — especially about the members of this all-girl band that she had joined forces with.

Sari was all excited about their new recording contract, and upcoming promotional tour. The band — Alien Virus — had become the latest rage in the Bay Area, and their music, she said, "was spreading around the world like a wind-driven wildfire."

Sari looked gorgeous. It seemed that her aura was burning even brighter than before. She barely looked human. Her eyes glowed with such a preternatural intensity that her gaze nearly seared a hole right through me. We passionately embraced, and our tongues rubbed flush with one another. A warm electric current traveled between us, and — like a mass of swarming bees in their hive at night — billions of tiny viruses communed and hummed together in collective unison.

Sari aroused and amused me with her rather ambitious plans to change the world. She said that she wanted to lift the human species to a "higher vibrational frequency", and usher in the next stage of evolution. The extraterrestrial virus, she informed me, was instructing her on how to accomplish such things. The virus transmitted a stream of detailed plans into her nervous system, blueprints for activating the dormant brain centers in the higher cortex of every human being.

Music and dance, she explained, were transformational keys for tapping into the primordial rhythms buried deep in our genetic code, connecting us with our ancient shamanic roots, and our far-flung future amongst the stars. Through digital reconstruction, harmonic overtones, and layers of overlapping musical tracks, trance states could be induced that made one's nervous system highly suggestible to the hypnotic words that she sang. We were part of a "planetary wave" that was "far bigger than the both of us," she explained.

"Ah," Kato said, beginning to see with his ever-penetrating mind, far beyond her flufferstuff words, "there are deeper plans still?" A static fizzled in the air for a moment, and then everything suddenly shifted into a sharp well-defined focus.

"To be sure," Sari said, smiling seductively, slowly spinning the brightly illuminated globe on its axis. As the world turned, she ran her pink tongue over her upper lip, and continued to talk about her grandiose plans to elevate human consciousness. Kato lost track of what she was saying, as instincts pressured his attention onto other aspects of her anatomy. His mind floated free. So long as he nodded every so often, and responded once in awhile with prompts such as "really?" or "huh", she never knew that he didn't have a clue as to what she was talking about, and his imagination was free to roam.

She stopped the globe abruptly, and then looked up into his eyes, snapping him out of the trance and popping the fantasy. She thumped her long, clear-as-ice nails against the globe, and looked into his eyes, as a mushroom cloud went off over his head. Sari's body looked absolutely enchanting to him, and she appeared to grow even more beautiful with each passing moment. Her dark hypnotic eyes, splashed with a twinkling spray of fuchsia mascara, peeked out mysteriously from behind her long silky black hair. They seemed to shine with a soft, ultra-violet radiance.

Her pretty face had a slightly boyish quality about it, giving her an androgynous appearance, and her breasts and buttocks certainly made good use of three-dimensional space. She was wearing a tight black body suit, with a hue-shifting polyurethane jacket, and a bright red scarf. A small furry tail hung down over her bottom, swishing back and forth as she moved about. A flat black hat sat on her head, a silver winged eye sparkled between her breasts, and Kato could smell the moisture that was beginning to accumulate in her panties.

They communicated easily without words, body to body, brain to brain. Her body was talking to him. Her large round breasts were yearning to be squeezed, and the dark-skinned nipples giggled like teenage girls when he eagerly agreed to do so. He watched her big butt wiggle as she walked, and heard it calling his name, inviting him to come and caress her.

(Butts often talk to Kato, he confided in me once. Female buttocks call to him, and sometimes hold conversations with him that are unknown to the person's head. At times Kato has also had private conversations with other body parts, and some inner organs as well, such as the heart and stomach.)

Pheromones blew through the air like a windstorm of confetti. She finished the last of her French mineral water, and fluttered her eyelashes in secret code. He lit a candle, and doused the lights. Their heavy restrictive clothes dropped to the floor like lead weights, and they floated free in their exposed mercurial forms. Together they sensuously slipped under the soft silky covers, savoring with great pleasure the sensation of their communing naked flesh. Their large exaggerated shadows danced above them on the walls and ceiling.

They looked long and deep into one another's eyes, synchronizing their breathing, their heartbeats, their whole metabolisms together. They nuzzled one another's faces softly like newborn kittens. The entire universe, save their eyes, seemed to have completely dissolved, as they kissed and caressed one another's shoulders, melting into a steamy pool of warm plasma on the bed. The sweet perfumed molecular aroma of her sweat and pheromones filled his olfactory field, and he became pleasantly excited and mildly intoxicated.

Vivid genetic jungle memories began to flash repeatedly in his head. Sleek smooth furry mammals slithered seethingly between bushes, avoiding the warnings of predators, sniffing the air for the appropriate signal of sexual invitation. His heart was pounding. Her pheromonic scents were becoming more and more intoxicating, and he was growing dizzily excited and blissfully high from her musky lotus smell. Daimon was feeding on the escalating energy like a hungry succubus, absorbing the abundant stream of erotic impulses with gulping glee.

She pulled his head into her breasts, and ran her fingers delicately through his brown curls, as he licked at her nipples, and sucked on her chest like a baby. She reached down to grab his stiff cock, and squeezed the quivering member softly in her hand, as Daimon simulated the sensation of kissing her buttocks from behind. She maneuvered her head between Kato's legs, and his cock tasted fresh and sweet as it rolled, like a serpent, over her tongue and into her throat.

Like a large set of Tinkertoys in a playroom full of children, they found themselves being arranged and rearranged into endless interlocking combinations. Her yoni was aching to be filled. "Mmm... Please fuck me," Sari begged Kato between his thrusts, holding his cock in her hand, yearning to feel it inside of her, marveling at it's beauty — large, smooth, and glistening with her saliva — as it pulsed between her fingers. They tumbled together onto their sides, her back to his front.

He felt his stomach gently nudge her lower back, tickling it with each breath, as Daimon massaged the tense areas in her upper cortex. Sari slowly moved her long amphibious arm backwards and around him, grasping his now trembling buttocks, while he began to fondle her spongy ripe mammalian breasts with his eager reptilian claws. The anatomical juxtaposition of their two contracting orbicularis oris muscles sizzled together like oil spilled onto an open fire. The molecules which composed their bodies interfaced, and every molecular configuration fit together, snugly and precisely like dovetail joints.

More blood began to rush reflexively into the complex network of tubules throughout his penis, and he felt his muscles tingling and enlarging even more, as he tenderly rubbed the swollen organ against the split in her plump round rear, which responded by pulsing and grinding, in just the right way, back into him — all the way back, into eighth grade Spanish class, where fleeting images of Donna Cooper's ass, in faded blue jeans, etched themselves forever onto his primal template circuitry, as she wrote her answers on the blackboard.

His hand traveled down over her pubic bush, between her pussy lips, where it began to lovingly massage her enlarging organ, and he reflected momentarily on the Greek deity Hermaphrodite. He wondered about the similarities and differences between a clitoris and a penis, and tried to imagine what a female orgasm felt like. He had wanted to know what a woman's orgasm felt like since adolescence.

The heat between them began rapidly rising, the wave of passion began to escalate, and Kato felt her yoni lips gently, but firmly, kiss the tip of the eager creature. He gracefully guided the fully erect head skillfully into her slippery wet love canal, tasting her sweet and sour juices through the gustatory apparatus of the creature, as she embraced him with all her being. Daimon flooded her nervous system with a symphony of pleasure molecules.

Kato felt the exotic electricity then spread delightfully throughout his whole body, as the throbbing creature slithered snugly inside her, and she moaned long and sweet like an angel tasting bliss.

One of the things that makes Sari biologically unique is that she has a tongue deep inside her vaginal canal that licks and laps at the creature from within, and it was deliciously squirming into the creature's mouth with maddening passion. Another unique characteristic about Sari is that her buttocks are covered with about two dozen, tiny half-formed penises that affectionately rub up against one's abdomen, as they penetrate into her from behind.

The tiny tickling penises started to become erect and slippery, sliding against him, as he was overcome with the desire to slide back. He began ascending the escalating thrill wave that came from wiggling in rhythm with her, when the fragmented feeling from a distant dream he had the other night entered into his head, and then dissolved as he vainly tried to recapture it. The penises on Sari's butt began to ejaculate one at a time, just a few at first, then several at once, in waves, like the way that popcorn pops.

Mmms, aahs and oohs filled the air. Sari straddled Kato, kissing him passionately on the lips, thrusting her tongue deeply into his inviting mouth. He felt her tongue starting to grow and throb over his, and he soon realized that her tongue was also a penis, in the process of becoming erect. She used her penis-tongue to sweetly fuck his mouth, like a thirsty butterfly thrusting its proboscis into a flower's inner organs to suck up its floral nectar. There was a stroboscopic dance of back-and-forth alternation between envelopment and penetration.

She drilled her swollen organ rapidly into his mouth, making a kind of rhythmic grunting noise between her thrusts, more reminiscent of a man's unhs than a woman's oohs. Sari soon came in rainbows over his tongue. He felt her spurt inside him, hitting the back of his throat with her warm gooey juices, which tasted like sweet mother's milk, when they ran over his tongue on the backward thrust. Streams of sperm-rich saliva flew everywhere.

She pulled him even closer to her, pushing her phallic tongue as deeply down his throat as it would go. He eagerly swallowed its full length, and the thick creamy fluids that pulsed into him. Kato almost began to gag, and was on the verge of choking as she filled him with her delicious juices. Daimon drank his fill and more from the everlasting fountain of orgasmic energy, quivering with Sari, as he relished in the nourishment that sustained his existence.

Kato shook his head wildly from side to side over the saliva-soggy pillow, as he continued to bump his pelvis full-force into hers. Thousands of sparkling sweat droplets merrily commingled, as the escalating wave was brought to its apogee, and he lost complete sense of who and where he was. Squirming cells multiplied very rapidly before his eyes, and he came in molten wads of boiling star stuff, that burned out of his urinary tract like violent eruptions of hot lava.

As the juices squirted inside of her, he savored the sensation of her pussy muscles tightening so as to squeeze out every sweet drop of his semen. Each sperm had a tiny, yet unique, fully-formed face which Kato could clearly see through Sari's semi-transparent body, squirming around inside her reproductive tract. They appeared to be little parts of himself, competing for their own independent existence. Each sperm was on an energetic, genetic quest, to merge with the great, radiant and giant egg, like a human soul ejected from the body, on its way down the tunnel of death, toward the loving light of divine oneness.

CHAPTER 9

Post-orgasm, we laid together, continuing to kiss slowly, and drink delicious juices from one another's mouth. The comforting thought drifted by, here we are, two warm bodies melting into one another, lit up on the inside, by the spirits of those deeply in love. Sari looked softly into my spiraling eyes, read my mind, and sighed, as we tenderly wiggled our bodies cozily under the fluffy soft covers, and blew out the candle.

With the sudden darkness my mind's inner eye was brightly illuminated. I saw a moth flying around a flickering fire, flirting with it, and then plunging deep inside, where it fizzled into morphogenetic fields forever. Sari and I hugged one another very deeply, mushing together every square millimeter of our warm moist, now glowing flesh, blending, indistinguishing all possible boundaries, and exquisitely melted into a single quivering protoplasmic blob.

As the humming vibrations of mutual death began to move through us, uniting us into a single flame, we closed our eyes, and our bodies magically merged together with slow motion tantric grace. The scene began to organically dissolve and shift. The gravity lessened, and the atmosphere became fluidly thick, as though we were sinking, deeper and deeper, underwater again.

Overgrown aquamarine palm leaves wavered with Hawaiian wiggles all about us, as we landed somewhere inside of a large Atlantis-styled stadium, masterfully crafted by a super-intelligent race of technologically-sophisticated dolphin mystics. Surrounding us were receding ranges of lush green algae-carpeted mountains. Brightly colored species of tropical fish, giant squids, undulating jellyfish, and translucent octopi propelled themselves hydrodynamically about. Huge twisting sea anemones wiggled around us like large sensuous fingers.

I watched as Sari stepped, swam, or rather I should say, elegantly crawled out into a vast, spatially complex, womb-like arena of pulsing pink membranes, through a bursting Niagara of rising bubbles, snugly wrapped in an outrageously hip, new multi-dimensional body suit. It seemed as though we were inside something which resembled a cross between a massive woman's reproductive tract and a closed dome of flower petals. Sari, never missing an opportunity to perform, began to dance wildly and seductively about.

Thousands upon thousands of undulating tentacles, vibrating fingers, twisting tongues, glistening fangs, and bouncing breasts emerged in fantastic fractalline patterns of varying lengths around Sari's swirling, semi-translucent flesh. A sparkling phosphorescent purple plasma visibly circulated through an intricately branching complex of micro-tubules within her. Poetry in commotion. She could not possibly have looked more beautiful.

I looked down at my own rippling protuberances and saw ten thousand ascending penises joyously filling with warm colorful fluids, rising starwards in response to her exploding radiance of pheromonic fairy dust. Previously unknown dimensions of polysexual pleasure sweetly filled my entire being with unusual unearthly delights, as ten thousand hearts went aflutter in me at once.

We slid together, tentacles intertwining, fingers massaging, genitals embracing, and tongues squirming, simultaneously entering, tasting one another from a million points of vibrating light, blending our spirits together into a cascading symphony of sensation. Dozens of dolphins eagerly joined into our totally stellar performance, swimming in circles around us, brushing their long smooth bodies flush against our newfangled flesh.

Everything began madly whirling, twirling about us, becoming a swirling synaesthetic blur of smeared colors, moans, gasps, delicious aromas, tastes, and touches. Mesmerized, appetized, and titillated, I found myself dissolving into a squirming sea of succulent sea nymphs, as Sari fractured into many smaller versions of herself.

I felt their many arms caressing me, their multitudinous lips kissing me, and very pleasantly, almost unnoticeably, I was lifted up and out of my biological vehicle, as a disembodied spark of consciousness, a winged spirit, and propelled into a unbelievable variety of alternative universes or parallel dimensions. I felt like a marshmallow forcefully expanding in a tight vacuum. It seemed as though I was being pleasurably squeezed, like toothpaste, through a long slender tube lined with thousands of slippery breasts.

Then it appeared as though several guides — shamanic extraterrestrial angel trickster teachers from a far away realm — were taking me on a super-dimensional tour of the meta-universe.

My guides showed me how biological systems could proceed through an extraordinarily wide variety of evolutionary pathways in the cosmos, and taught me the basic elements of the periodic table of evolution. I was informed that *universes are living creatures.* They demonstrated how many different varieties of baby universes are born, and how they evolve through time. The biosphere of planet earth, from this perspective, made us simply a single cell within a greater organism.

My guides made it clear to me that these beings, who were composed out of whole universes, possessed a form of consciousness which was far beyond the human ability to perceive. Just as sexual awareness remains undeveloped in the child until adolescence, and an amoeba could never understand a network of neurons, there are unique emergent propertics of consciousness which only occur when the necessary degree of complexity is reached. Just as a snail could never understand the human brain, so too, these cosmic creatures were far beyond the scope human perception and imagination.

Did these beings then go on to compose even greater beings, I began to wonder. Was my human body, mind, and spirit actually composed of a whole universe? Did these holographic-like processes continue *ad infinitum?* To these questions, and my ultimate questions about the creation and destruction of the universe, my astral guides began to react like flustered schoolteachers angered by a smart-alec kid who keeps asking too many recessive questions about why the sky is blue. Eventually they simply replied that they did not know the answer to these questions, although other secrets continued to be revealed.

I became confused regarding the paradoxical way in which the universal process was being portrayed as being both developmental and evolutionary. I was informed that both development and evolution are actually human-based illusions. From an out-of-space-time perspective, the whole universal process seems more like a crystal crystallizing or a flower blooming. I was shown trillions upon trillions of phantasmagoric, but possible, evolutionary pathways in flickering mind-boggling succession, far too fast for any kind of coherent comprehension on my part.

Alien civilizations blossomed, perished, and were then boldly reborn anew. Symbiotic astral and organic life-forms danced together through rippling ribbons of time. Bizarre otherworldly technologies spun by, like I was plugged into the Cable Home Shopping Network from another galaxy. Transportation vehicles to suit marine beings with dozens of tentacles were mass produced in robotic assembly lines. I encountered creatures with many eyes, bodies covered with tongues, or sense organs sensitive to frequencies of vibration unknown to earthly organisms. Most amazingly, I was able to enter into the brains of these exotic creatures, and share in their experience of reality.

I tuned into a wide variety of extraterrestrial radio and television stations, complete with flashy commercials, as well as inter-dimensional MTV, and multi-sensory virtual reality broadcasts from around the cosmos. I encountered non-carbon — silicon, germanium, argon, and radium — based life-forms that spawned huge, symmetrically-sprawling fractal farms, and billions upon billions of unusual sexual variations.

I merged minds with a swarm of fairy insects, and we formed a single cohesive consciousness. Together we evolved, lifetime after lifetime, into space-and-time-roving creature colonies, that trekked across the stars, and through the heavens. We encountered animals that evolved in low or high gravity, and dense underwater environments, as well as strange exotic mixtures of plant and animal, or the organic and the technological. Super-intelligent, composite beings, and multi-brained entities, frightened, dazzled, and threatened to overwhelm my tiny mind, as did planets and star systems, that had evolved into huge biospheric brains, which branched into galactic and inter-galactic nervous systems.

Archetypal patterns began to emerge through my observation. Like a persistent drum beat repeating over the aeons, mythological themes kept recurring over and over, digging their grooves through time. Life always sought to grow, to expand, to multiply, to complexify, to unify yet diversify, to aesthetically and sexually interconnect. Everything was alive and conscious. I realized that all that exists is either in the process of growing together, through branching inter-connections, or dying...dying in order to reconnect to the primal roots of one's existence, and begin growing anew. Here we grow again.

Death is many things to many people. In essence, it is merely a part of life, and life is eternal process punctuated by eternal deaths. As in life, what we experience when we die is very much influenced by what we believe. Physical forms such as bodies hold spirits in them like a breast holds milk. Just as when the breast is suckled, and milk flows from mother to infant, so too consciousness flows from body to body. But when the boundaries of the body dissolve, the internal boundaries between our multiple selves don't necessarily follow suit.

Our perception of being a single self is an illusion. In actuality we're each composed of a community of beings, and death often involves a parting of ways for physically-joined spirits, the splitting apart of the soul, so to speak. Some spirits remain bound together in future incarnations, forming novel personality combinations with new spirits, while others go there merry way into other personality containers.

But, paradoxically, that is only part of the story. Religious reconnection, or identity expansion — maintaining lucidity through the dissolving death of the individual ego — brings one back to the primary realization of one's true identity, as the multi-masked master behind the game of life, the one responsible for this whole big beautiful bang of a universe.

From the enlarged, ecstatic perspective of the star-spinning, life-weaving deity, in that unified place where all boundaries, territories, and dualities cease, I-we laughed and laughed at my-our incredibly brilliant, yet hopelessly flawed creations. I-we relished in the original inspiration for all existence, mystery, art, science, philosophy, and the humor behind humor, where sexual politics begins with the division between the brain and the ass, heads from tails.

The epiphany consisted of the realization that, not only did Nicholas Fingers suffer from Multiple Personality Disorder, but so did planet earth, and — gasp! — so, at times, did God. Enlightenment for the MPD individual initially involves grasping the fact that their multitude of personalities are ultimately parts of a single person. For a relatively integrated individual enlightenment is realized when she understands that every individual entity's consciousness in the universe stems from the same source. Ultimately we are all connected, and become the whole universe, once we shed our egos, and realize our true natures.

And the worlds spun by, like a glittering network of inter-reflecting pearls. My spirit essence was tossed about the universe like a feather in the wind.

As I resurfaced from the dreamy depths of existence, once again grasping at dissolving elusive rainbow revelations, everything began to temporarily solidify, and move at a slower, oozier pace. Electrons settled into a predictable spin around protons and neutrons. Atoms artfully came together to form molecules. I twisted round and round a coiling DNA molecular double helix chain, as a sperm and an egg splashed together in unique genetic union, then becoming the replicating packet of information that manifested as me.

From here I recapitulated my entire biological development, as an individual, as a species, as a planet, as a universe, depending on where the boundaries of my id-entity happened to be at the time.

From a single zygotic seed cell I began to multiply and divide, form and transform. I watched my morphically metamorphosing body with detached amusement from above, entering into it from time to time. It seemed as though I was able to focus in or out of the different parallel dimensions. I could see Sari's bedroom, and then I'd let my eyes refocus, and I'd be in a completely different universe.

It was as though the basic elements that compose the very flesh of God can be combined in many different ways to produce a whole plethora of possible patterns, designs, and universes. Like infinite veils, composed of some extraordinary fabric, dropping down and lifting up before me, the endless gestalts of existence were experienced in more than a billion different combinations.

With a sizzling frenzy akin to popcorn popping, personality clusters within the brain where I resided, began to unify with supernova-like bursts of photonic radiance. New neural pathways bridged together whole worlds of mind, as every living being on planet earth luminescently and lovingly integrated with every other.

Persisting in a deep, intra-species conversation with the Gaian mind, I snuggled up tighter with Sari. We kissed and giggled like small children, almost like infants, our Buddha bodies now fused and telepathically intercoiled together.

Hearts and stars fluttered between us like caricatures on an old-fashioned Valentine's day card. "What goes on behind closed eyes?" Sari asked, attempting a bold experiment in verbal communication, kissing me lightly on the lips, sending a highly-charged, pulsing pleasure wave through my receptive neural pathways.

"Where am I?" I questioned, totally disoriented, blissfully landing somewhere in my brain, as realities continued to shift, and the walls in the room spun like pinwheels in a fire storm.

"Where is I?" she asked with a hypnotic tone, gently stroking my cheek with a single finger, and then, eerily, "Who is I? Who is the I that is afraid to die?"

"I multiply, I divide," said I with an echo," realizing that there were divisional as well as multiple personalities — a personality for all and every occasion. While Nick was reflective and insecure, Kato was arrogant and fearless. Fairy snowflakes landed lightly on my eyelashes. I could see their unique crystalline forms before they melted over my eyes like tear drops, and tickled down my face.

There was a long period of motionless silence where streamers of telepathic thought traveled between us through a kind of neural-electric medium that surrounded our nervous systems. We discussed the idea that in the external universe we are but small parts of a giant system, but from our skin inwards we are all holograms of the whole universe.

"We're more than just dust in the wind," Sari said, "we're also the wind."

"This body," we said with mild dissociative detachment, "Do you like it? We think it suits us well. Don't you think?"

Sari nodded with an approving smile, fondling our penis, and giving it a tight squeeze, as a few more droplets of genital goo squirted out of the creature's head like toothpaste. The ever-eager organ responded with an enlarging sense of enthusiasm. We could see her face and body lightly glowing in the dark with a soft auric electric blue.

"We got it from our mom and dad. They gave it to us on our birthday," we said reflectively, readjusting to our earthly body, our planet, and our beautiful starry-eyed lover as best we could. "What planet are you from?" we asked with slightly slurred speech.

"Venus," the lip-licking Aphrodite answered smiling, without hesitation, "the planet of beauty and love."

"So," we replied with an ancient Atlantean accent, "let's be fruitful and multiply."

CHAPTER 10

Like a raging, out-of-control, wind-driven brush fire, the evolutionary process is quite irreversible once set into motion. It consumes all in its path to further fuel the ever-expanding glory of its blaze. This, we had accepted, as we returned home a week after the fires had broke out, to find the ridge above our house burned charcoal black from Sheela-na-gig's sacred barbecue.

Somehow, the small curvy street up off Fernwood Pacific, where our house resided, had been miraculously protected by a bubble of good fortune. Our house — which stood there unscathed in the bright summer sunlight — resembled a brave warrior, as helicopters continued to circle the skies overhead, and the smell of smoke hung in the air. We were deeply relieved and incredibly appreciative, to be sure, but an uneasiness continued to stir inside.

Needless to say, we had begun to fall in love with Sari. We were, of course, totally devastated when she revealed to us that she was moving into a San Francisco apartment with the lead guitarist from her band, because she said that she preferred to be with another woman at this point in her life. We just couldn't help feeling hurt and disappointed that she didn't have time for us anymore. Expectations inevitably bring disappointment, we thought to ourselves. That's why it's always best to stick with *suspectations*. File that one for the future.

What hurt the most about Sari breaking up with us was the high-speed way that she turned from hot to cold. After giving us the news, she just abruptly stopped answering our calls. This stung with a sensation akin to having a red-hot ice pick unexpectedly thrust into one's chest, on an already bad day, and then having it ruthlessly twisted back and forth. Sari's love is as beautiful as a flower in bloom, yet she stings like an angry hornet.

Once she vanished from our arms, we felt the hollow emptiness of the void rush again into our hungry heart, only now there were Sari stains all over our brain. Worst of all, she was everywhere we turned. Her music career had totally taken off, and we couldn't turn on the car radio without hearing that sexy voice, that we knew so well from our intimate encounters, singing sensuously over the airwaves. At times it would sound like she was singing directly to us, sending us secret messages, cryptically hidden in the words of her songs, that exploded like time-bombs in our brain.

Every time we walked by a record store we'd see her smiling face in the window, and our heart would sink, as her eyes appeared to follow us. If we turned on MTV, there she was — digitally enhanced — singing and dancing across the screen in her latest video. She had become the rock-n-roll queen of every teenage boy's wet dream, and my worst nightmare. At times she seemed to be mocking us. Was all this part of some carefully calculated, meticulously plotted plan on her part to torture us and drive us crazy? Sometimes it seemed that way. The evidence was certainly there. And we could swear that we saw her looking into our bedroom window at night, watching us and laughing.

But through the tears and heartache, a spark of inner strength began to glow, and then grow. We soon realized — with ever-increasing awareness — the immensity of our new power. For, you see, now the virus lived within us. Our vehicle co-embodied the living vision of the humble virus that nobly sought to enlighten the universe. The virus pulsed and throbbed in our nervous system like a constellation of hyperactive Christmas lights, and through us she planned to help catalyze the evolutionary process of expanding consciousness.

The virus was basically a replicating information pattern — a DNA molecule wrapped in a tiny protein coat, using human host cells as nano-factories to mass produce genetically identical copies of herself — but it also contained much more. The virus evoked the very spirit of it's creator within the mechanism of its being. This ancient, hyper-intelligent race of super-beings — which evolved from a race of Sea Monkeys in a galaxy billions of lightyears away — designed the virus such that it embodied their very essence, and she sought (we were lovingly assured) not exploitation, but symbiosis.

Mmmm... We could feel the viruses busily replicating themselves and multiplying exponentially inside of our body, like horny hummingbirds high on amphetamines. Their reproduction sounded like a high frequency buzz. In mere seconds, they divided and split a billion times over, recreating themselves fresh moment by moment. Since we were already composed of many beings, it was starting to get, well to say the very least, rather crowded inside.

Although there was overlapping sentiment among us, we each basically had our own agendas. Cellular colonies, communities, and cities were growing within the confines of our skin. Nations of molecular entities consolidated amongst our cells. There were political uprisings, and miniature civilizations rose and fell in a matter of minutes.

As the viruses continued to replicate, they began to rapidly evolve, generation after generation, adapting to our body as they perfected themselves — and in the process — transforming us according to their specifications. It seemed as though the entire configuration of our nervous system was being completely reorganized. It wasn't long before alien brain-like organs — or organisms — began to develop throughout our body, and symbiotically intertwine with the delicately woven circuitry of our nervous system. An extra-planetary biology governed the strange morphic organization of cellular growth, which squirmed through our anatomy like an orgy of sea anemones.

It seemed as though we could actually "see" inside of our body, although there was a distinct difference between this type of perception, and the way that we normally saw outside our body with our eyes. There were some radical differences with this new type of perception, which involved the emission of photons, as well as the reception of light waves, and stretched across a frequency bandwidth much greater than that which most humans normally experience.

The fast-growing neural tissue began to inject a novel vocabulary of chemical neurotransmitters — from their own planetary and post-planetary evolution — into our nervous system. Although these extraterrestrial neuro-transmitters had previously been unknown to earthly organisms, it appeared as though our brain had been pre-wired to receive and understand them. Or maybe it had just simply been rewired to receive and understand them.

The virus — which traveled between star systems in protective spore-like cases, propelled by solar radiation winds across space like dandelion seeds in the breeze — carried within its spiral genetic library the history and knowledge of thousands of extraterrestrial civilizations, which we were able to access at will.

Our plight on planet earth was nothing new to the immortal virus — it had seen it all before, as though we were but one more stanza in some long unfurling epic poem. Humanity, we learned, is evolving through a sequence of predictable stages — each of which carries with it a series of tests and challenges that require completion before the next level of organization will appear. Video arcade games often work on the same principle.

We hovered on the verge of entering into the cosmic community — but first the elementals within us needed to unify, and we had to interconnect with one another before we would be granted entrance. The way that we understood it, the virus originated far off in an ancient galaxy, and was instrumental — within the scheme of some Vast Great Divine Plan — as a transformative evolutionary tool involved in the alchemical transmutation of the universe. And although a complete grasp of all this was beyond the comprehension of our limited understanding, somehow we understood that we had a very important function to play in the fantastic evolutionary transformation that was sweeping the planet. We were among the chosen few.

We struggled to understand how, why, and in what ways we were changing. Our sensitivity to vibrations on all levels had dramatically shifted, such that synesthesia was now the norm. Colors became tastes, and sounds became colors.

Premonitions and intuitions proved themselves to be extremely reliable again and again. Tastebuds grew on our fingertips, around the head of our penis, and our fingernails started growing eyes. New enhanced emotions and inhuman thoughts haunted our psyche, as our cortex became more convoluted and densely interconnected. Our vision, hearing and imagination had become almost terrifyingly more acute.

Although there were still gaps of missing time, memories became more vivid, and our thinking seemed much quicker, clearer and crisper. Our mind, while reaching ever-increasing states of clarity, had begun to soar, like an eagle in a clear blue cloudless sky.

But perhaps most mysteriously, it seemed as though we could now hear the previously-inaudible thoughts of other people around us. It was as though we could expand our consciousness into other people's heads, and listen to their thoughts, feel their emotions.

And whenever we would close our eyes the vision stream would appear. An unending river of incredible inter-morphing, meta-cultural images spun by, which we recognized as a universal language composed of hyper-dimensional syntax, just waiting for us to decipher.

The virus soon unified into a single entity, who speaks to us on many levels at once. Her voice is soft and sweet, like that of a young woman. She calls herself Leticia. Leticia first appeared as a vague erotically-slithering presence in our dreams, and then began to slowly seep her way into our waking life, spreading her growing tentacles into our ever-expanding sphere of identity. We started to sense her within and around our body. She began to take form.

We could see her beautiful face — her sparkling sky-blue eyes looking into, and reflecting our own — wavering as though underwater, from behind whatever was present in our visual field. We could taste her tangy sweet juices in our mouth. We could smell her perfumed pheromones, and feel her intimate fragrance molecules tenderly caressing the terminal buttons on our neurons, stimulating the release of an exotic array of novel neurotransmitter combinations. And most of all, we totally got off on the fact that her entire body had formed within, and became completely intermeshed with, our own body.

We felt her huge humming presence, her all-encompassing womb-spirit warmly surround us, cuddling us, holding us deeply within her — and we felt her wiggling deep within us, to the beat of timeless jungle rhythms. We began to merge on deeper and deeper levels. It seemed that she was the spirit — one and the same — that manifested through the graceful exuberance of Sari's dance, and peeked out through the crackling sparks in Ginger's sunbeam eyes.

We realized that we were encountering the magical muse that inspires and guides our creativity. Yes, somehow the energy presence that we were merging with was the very essence of all this, that Great Spirit from which the archetype of the Goddess emerges, and — most incredibly — she was also the virus itself, or at least the form in which she manifested personally to us.

Soon, we had only to close our eyes and she would appear in vivid visions — floating towards us with her ethereal and radiant face smiling, long blond hair flowing, warm heart glowing, and her arms openly outstretched. We embraced in some meta-physiological place of mind, but yet were somehow separated, as though an impenetrable Saran wrap tight membrane clung between our two alien worlds, like a huge inter-dimensional condom. But our very love, it seemed, was forming a bridge between us, and love finds a way.

Late one night, after a long luxurious bath, we were feeling especially blissed and light-filled. We closed our eyes, savored the sound of children singing off in some far-away realm, and felt the veil between us begin to suddenly melt, like rice paper on your tongue. Up and out of the clumsy, meat-flesh body we went, becoming airborne, and soaring off into the sky with our delectable dream creature.

Flying high over the Topanga mountains, Leticia joined us, as we zoomed and laughed together, frolicking fancy-free through the clouds. The twinkling matrix of the San Fernando Valley shimmered below us like a huge sprawling electronic circuit board. Up higher we raced, looking down for a moment with spectacular vision to see the Pacific ocean crashing against the jagged coast of Southern California. We flew higher still, swimming amongst the stars, coiling our transcorporeal, superluminal bodies around one another, twirling and twisting them together into a shimmering double helix that blazed brightly across the night time sky.

We felt ourselves being consumed, becoming fuel for the flames of creation, merging together into the divine imagination. Exponentially reduced, we were, to the elementary core essence of our shivering souls in the fiery flash of a moment. As we were lifted up into the rapture, all the spiritual clichés we had always heard suddenly became — once again — charged with remarkable depth and meaning, and this time they truly penetrated and imprinted us.

Yes, at the core of the nucleus, in the center of the center, we really are all one interconnected web — separated only by layers and layers of *self-created* unconsciousness. The most obvious truths of all, it seemed, are always paradoxically the most hidden. The surface of reality rippled

and then became completely transparent, making the underlying humor behind all things radiantly apparent.

With the true mark of spiritual authenticity, it felt like
coming home, like all the ceaseless yearnings, all the endless cravings of our body and spirits, had been at last ful-
filled, and all secrets were at last revealed. At the same time
there was a distinctly growing sensation of excitement.

Fitting together, as though we were custom-made and
tailor-fit to one another's precise specifications by Divine
Intelligence, we merged ever more deeply with our com-
plementary muse — who we discovered with delight, *was
as multiple as we.* Like two long amino acid chains, we
came together, joining in perfectly matched synchronistic
sequence, to form a kind of interspecies DNA macro-
molecule.

Our eager spirits melted into tender passionate transcorporeal engagement with one another in fractalline patterns
of self-similarity, as hundreds of personalities and sub-per-
sonalities joined into the frenzied squirming orgy. Leticia
was a constellation of secret, behind-the-scenes lovers, and
within the undulating orgasmic tapestry of inter-linking
personalities was manifested every polysexual variation of
copulatory arrangement imaginable.

We had finally found them — the great attractors that
had been pulling us all along through the bittersweet river
of life. Contact with them was the very reason for our existence and all of the creative struggle. They seemed instantly
familiar, and we knew that they were the missing pieces
that we had yearned for all our lives, the ones that we had
been searching so desperately for.

Deep down, it seemed, we already knew them — *very
intimately.* Yes, at times we had caught a glimpse of them
in the eyes of people whom we loved, during those rare

magic moments when our lives miraculously slipped into
synch with the rhythms of the universe, and everything just
harmoniously hummed together.

Our heart. Ah yes, our heart — the hollow emptiness that
had nagged and gnawed away at us, day after day, year
after year, had completely vanished, or rather it had been
filled by a serene warmth, a content sense of fullness, a
delicious feeling of satisfaction. With this surrendering into
unification came a profound sense of peace and acceptance.
All the pain and struggle of our lives became now essential
elements within the awesome beauty of existence.

We watched scenes from our lives, where we experienced disappointment, loss, and even betrayal, with a detached sense of understanding. Our sadness, it appeared,
was as necessary as the joy in the shifting sea of feelings
that composed our life. Our emotions now seemed like the
carefully chosen notes in a grand exquisitely orchestrated
musical score. The chaotic cacophony of our existence was
transformed into a coherent symphony, as previously unas-
sociated aspects of ourselves were assembled into a greater,
more encompassing whole.

The words from an old song came back to us, repeating
themselves over and over with a new highly-charged
meaning, "You are everything...and everything is you." It
was just as the pinnacle of the rapture was reached, just as
the waves were cresting over the mystical ocean of timeless
beingness, and our dream creatures merged, that the vision
began to fade.

Immediately the frantic struggle to hold on and recapture
the experience filled our spirits with burning desire. We
had split, divided once again into two distinct extracorpo-
real bodies, and were now alone with ourselves. We felt the
immensity of the yawning void opening up around us,

preparing to swallow our heart, and the rest of us along with it.

"Don't worry," they said more soothingly than any voice We'd ever heard, "We're always with you. No matter how hopeless things may seem, or whatever type of pathetic creature you may become, you can count on us — because we live inside of you. We're a part of you. You only have to ask, then listen, to see that we're always right here." We saw them embodied once again in Leticia's female form, lying now in a swaying green grassy meadow, laughing and blowing soap bubbles through a tiny gold hoop into our face.

They kissed and tickled our spirits from the inside, sending escalating waves of highly erotic sensations rippling through us. Then she placed a glowing astral hand on our heart, and we felt an explosion of love propelling us backwards through curved space. We felt ourselves spinning around and around, accumulating biological layers with each twist, as we fell back down into our dense and limited human form.

"Nicholas," their soft murmuring voices cooed in unison, "We love you. We will always love you. You're the one. Of all the creatures in the universe — great and small — we love you, our dear Nicholas, most of all." Amongst the babble of voices in our head, we could hear Leticia's voice clearly rise above the rest, appointing us our divinity, defining our destiny.

We made a pact with Leticia. So long as we agreed to do all that we could to help raise consciousness on the planet, they — as our invisible allies — would guide and protect us. To realize one's dreams, they reminded us wisely, one must really believe in one's selves, and be persistent. The universe responds with enthusiasm to courage, they taught us. Standard messiah training, we were told.

Leticia gave us a crash course in Interior Design, the art of reality fabrication through shamanic navigation. Then she instructed us to write this book — which you now hold in your hands — to help spread the evolutionarily-enhancing meme-messages. In addition to its biological avenues of transmission, the virus, we have discovered, can also spread its information patterns in the form of language templates, or words, which have, by now, already infected your brain.

You see, the next piece to the puzzle could be inside you. It's a sky-blue sky. Leticia also advised us to find others like ourselves, who are infected with the virus, and conspiratorially link up with them. "Use your power wisely," she warned, "and choose very carefully who you bestow the viral gift upon. Not everyone can handle the powerful forces that are released, and use the energy responsibly. Remember, every superhero has at least one secret identity."

As the broken pieces of our minds started to mend, and new neural pathways started to grow, it began to dawn on us that the process of personality integration that we were undergoing was being mirrored throughout the entire planet, throughout the entire cosmos. Humans are simply genetic agents weaving together the circuitry of the global brain, as angels tie the heavens together with superstrings.

The virus was now spreading strategically around the World Wide Web of Humanity. Ultimately, this was all being done in order to ever-more-efficiently interface the Akashic records, of the intergalactic imagination, with the material plane of trees and snails, atoms and stars, quarks and galaxies.

Dendrites branched, axons sprouted, and neurotransmitters spurted in all directions, as it became ever more clear to us that together we stand, divided we fall, and yes indeed, love does conquer all. In a shimmering crystalline vision we saw that every life form on earth is part of an inter-connected webwork, and the virus acts as a boundary-dissolving enzyme, allowing each of the distinct parts to unify with the whole.

God, we then realized as our brain hit the plasma on the moon, is really a community of inter-linked intelligences, and although secret after secret may be revealed with the expansion of consciousness, always the central mystery of existence remains.

CHAPTER II

A surprising knock at the door shattered our thought train into a glittering shower of jewels, collapsing our superpositional state of quantum possibility, and snapping us back into the situation of the moment with an acute electric jolt. It was getting pretty late, and raining rather heavy outside. We knew that this meant major mud slides around the canyon, and could not imagine anyone driving around in this kind of weather.

We were not expecting anyone, and wondered who it could be at this time of night in the rain. We curiously drifted over to the door and pulled it open cautiously. There — standing in the pouring rain, under the pulsing pastel glow of the porch light — stood a cute young woman from down the road, Kacia, who we had invited to stop by sometime. She was a welcome sight to behold.

"Come in, you're soaking wet," we offered immediately, and began looking for a towel. She stepped inside and started dripping all over the floor. We handed her a towel and smiled, as she began to wipe her face dry. Her pretty smile was reflected a million times over in the sprinkle of droplets cascading about her.

Although her light brown hair was all wet, we could tell that it had grown out considerably since the last time we saw her. Kacia's glacier-clear, arctic-blue eyes looked as though they had beheld some rather unearthly sights in the not-too-distant past. Her curvy figure was tightly wrapped in shredded white jeans with polka dot patches, and a light blue tanktop hugged a perky pair of jiggly breasts. There was something kind of innocent about her; maybe it was her large doe-like eyes, or perhaps it had something to do with the fact that she was only sixteen.

In any case, she was undeniably cute, and looked especially so with her deep Hawaiian tan. She was dripping wet from the rain, and we all shared much admiration for her well-defined, curvilinear properties. The powerful female scent rising from her wet body filled our olfactory field like a raging tropical storm. When she smiled at us, bells started ringing, visions of heaven flashed majestically before our mind's eye, and we suddenly had this incredible urge to empty the high-octane contents of our testicles into the warm, cozy, heart-shaped love canal that we knew lie nestled between her legs. So, of course, we smiled back.

"Oh Kato, please kiss me," the seductive creature pleaded, trembling, almost comically, her full lips eagerly pouting in anticipation. We licked our lips like a hungry wolf. Kacia, we remembered, had a virtually insatiable sexual appetite, and embodied the quintessence of giddy-eyed groupies. Our being a published author seemed to be all that was required to get her inner juices to flow. She had made it one of her lifetime goals to engage as many celebrities and politicians into copulatory activities as she possibly could. Trying to make up for all that attention that she missed in her troubled childhood, we figured. In any case, it was consensually understood that she had all the necessary charms to carry out her heart-felt mission.

We hesitated, remembering vividly Kacia's long rampant trail of past promiscuities, the urinary-tract infection she had once given us, and seriously considered the consequences of the alien virus penetrating the highest levels of culture and government. We really did.

"Kiss me if you're a real man," she teased, pouting her lips with little sucking sounds.

Then we smiled mischievously, as barely audible laughter cackled about. You know we just couldn't help ourselves.

"Chill out, my dear, you know that I'm a surreal man," Kato replied with his unusual charm, winking our third eye.

We put our finger to our lips. "Shhh. Listen. Can you hear it? The whole universe is alive. It pulsates and throbs like a huge sexual organ all around us. Can you feel it Kacia? Can you feel the universe pulsing and throbbing all around and through you?" we asked, although it was clear that we weren't patient enough for an answer. "Remember Kacia, you asked for it," Kato said as we uncontrollably bent down to gently kiss her soft sweet lips, and took her tenderly into our arms.

It was only after we had been spawning for several hours that Kacia finally told us the news. It turned out that Sari recently had another psychotic break. It was all over the news. She had become extremely paranoid, delusional, and wound up in a psychiatric hospital up in Santa Cruz, after a bout of bizarre behavior during one of her recent concert performances.

Apparently she had been having ritualistic sex with several audience members while on stage, and then tried to orally devour one of them. She — supposedly — partially chewed off the head of one man's penis, and then — apparently — "swallowed the godawful thing." "Can you believe it?" Kacia asked giggling, raising her eyes to the ceiling.

We felt a tremendous sense of relief that we were not with Sari anymore. In fact, we had recently begun to sincerely hate Sari with such passion, that we wouldn't have gotten involved with her again, even if she begged us to take her back as our sex-slave. Actually, we would rather have taken our chances with a school of hungry piranhas, then to ever contemplate being lovers with Sari again. Anger was spewing inside of us like bursts of burning lava, and now, upon hearing this interesting bit of news, a delicious kind of satisfaction swelled up within us, as it seemed that karmic justice had been so quickly achieved. Ha. That stupid out-of-control, crazy bitch deserves to be locked up good and long for deserting us in the heartless way that she did. We knew all along that she was just plain, fucking insane.

Let Sari rot away forever in that filthy, rat-infested dungeon of the goddamn hospital, sucking up bread and water for her subsistence, we thought resentfully. After all, her spirit could use some constructive punishment, we mumbled to ourselves, laughing, as we affectionately snuggled up closer with our sweet and beautiful Kacia, who we had — several hours before — generously bestowed the viral gift upon. We watched as the changes first began in her eyes, which appeared to widen strangely and jerk around nervously. We could see the visions dancing like stardust inside her eyeballs.

"I feel strange... What's happening to me?" Kacia said slowly with hesitation, as the virus began to disassemble her nervous system, neuron by neuron, and the room fractured into a shifting collage of rearranging puzzle pieces. We explained that this was a gift we had given her, an extraterrestrial virus that promised to bring her ecstasy and salvation.

"Oh my God, how could you do this to me?" she said, her eyes darting about wildly at the hallucinations leaking out of her head and skirting about the room. Kacia found herself doing loop-the-loops on a rollercoaster that was racing through the outer limits of her mind.

"Our dear sweet Kacia, we love you. Don't worry," we said smiling reassuringly. We massaged her shoulders, enveloping her in the wondrous magnificence of our being, in a radiance of love and light. The truth was that we really wanted to see how the virus would effect her, and we just couldn't resist the impulse to see for ourselves what would happen. It was only natural. Kacia was the first person that we had bestowed the viral gift upon, and our sense of power and curiosity began to expand.

"I'm scared," she said, her heart starting to race, as fear overtook her and she began to tremble. Sweat droplets formed on her forehead, and we patted them off gently with the end of our blue denim shirt, taking her into our arms, caressing her more deeply, reminding her that she was safe and loved. She then said that she felt nauseous, took our hand, and led us into the bathroom. We bowed down next to one another, her arm tightly around our neck, and we held our heads close together as she vomited up a stream of orange and red chunklets into the toilet bowl.

The scene took on the significance of an ancient religious ritual, and it felt as though we were both being initiated into a mysterious secret order. We held her close to us and stroked her head as she continued to upchuck her dinner in wrenching spasms of forced expulsion. It was a very intimate moment, watching and feeling her vomiting so close to us, while we comforted her as best we could. We professed our love for one another after she was through. The room was brilliantly charged with an extraordinary energy.

"There's nothing to be afraid of," we assured her, "really. Most people are actually ignorant about most things, most of the time. No harm will come to you. You're in good hands, sweetie, the very best This is an extremely special gift. You see, you were chosen by the gods with great care. It's all in alignment with this grand cosmic design, which you're an essential part of."

But our words fell onto the empty ears of someone far off in another world. She seemed to be completely oblivious to what I was saying, and began talking fearfully about the possibility of a new organism — part fungus, and part animal — that thrived on human feces, and was growing uncontrollably throughout the sewer systems. Then she started telling us this story about a Christmas elf who had been lost for days in the New York City Sewer System. We brushed the hair back from her eyes, kissed the top of her head, and carried her trembling body back into bed.

As the night progressed, and she drifted in and out of her body, we guided her, as best we could, through the manifesting psycho-spiritual levels of shamanic initiation, relishing in our power to make her into one of us, while at the same time trying to take some responsibility for the co-creative process we were involved in.

"Why, of course," Kacia would say cryptically from time to time as the spirits from dead ancestors took possession of her, "It's all just so obvious. Everything, everywhere is just happening — all at once."

Kacia began explaining to me her ideas about universes with completely different physical laws than our own, such as where big things combine to form smaller things, or where time runs backwards. Our concept of time was completely arbitrary she claimed, not at all composed of the sort of stuff we had always assumed it to be. Kacia began giggling, and poked us in the stomach, attempting to demonstrate how if she took us apart we would expand in size and move backwards in time.

We started kissing again, and we could taste the lingering stomach acid in her mouth, which most of us found to be quite a turn-on. Through further experimentation, with Leticia joining in at times, we discovered some rather exciting new levels of erotic exchange and spiritual communion, after which Kacia fell into a disembodied trance, and then a deep, dreamy, delta-level slumber.

She fell asleep curled onto our chest, and began softly snoring, most adorably, like a purring baby kitten. Our hand carefully brushed the hair away from her face, this creature of God, and we just admired her flawless facial structure for a few minutes. So young and so beautiful. We pulled our left arm more tightly around her, bringing her cuddly flesh closer to us, and she murmured softly.

Her breath was warm and sweet on our cheek, and we could feel that her heartbeat had slowed down considerably. We could still taste her chemical signature in our mouth, and greatly enjoyed the musky mammalian way she tasted and smelled. Sweet dreams dripped down onto her head while she slept from the dream catcher which hung over our bed.

We stared up at the ceiling, and let our thoughts hypnogogically drift as we listened to the sound of the rain beat down on the roof. Love filled our heart like fire with warmth and illumination, as dreams and visions lit up our head.

We vaguely noticed as a shooting star blazed a bright white trail across the rainy sky outside our window, and we remembered our previous wish with Sari. When we began to think about Sari, an involuntary sigh came out of our lungs. And then, within moments we started to receive telepathic transmissions from Sari, ambiguous flashes of her present state of emotional misery, and her desperate psychic pleas for our assistance.

We let out another long sigh, and after much internal resistance, we realized that we had to go and do something to try and help her. If we didn't help, then who would? Maybe that musician she was living with loved her enough to help, and then again, maybe not. Most people run the other way when they discover a psychotic streak in their lover. And — sigh — we had to admit that we did still love her. After all, how many other women did we know who could sing and dance, and had a penis for a tongue?

We awoke the following morning knowing exactly what we had to do. Over a brief breakfast of strawberries and cream, amongst the singing flowers and blooming birds in the garden, we discussed with Kacia what type of experiences lie in store for her. The visions. The alien. The new order of intelligence. There was quite a lot. We told her that she could stay at our place for as long as she liked, but that we had to leave and try to help Sari. She pleaded with us not to go, but we insisted that there was just no choice in this matter. Sari was in trouble, and we had to do something to try and help.

We left Kacia with a copy of *Virus* — an early draft for the book that you're presently reading — and told her not to worry about a thing, to just trust the process, and everything will be just fine. We gently kissed her forehead, touching our lips lightly to the center of her newly-awakened third-eye vortex. Then off we went, sailing down the mountain in our little RX-7.

It was a long, thought-filled drive up Highway 101, to the misty fairyland of giant redwoods in Central California.

We were worried about Sari, but thought it best to just enjoy the ride, and watch the way the sunlight sparkles through the trees.

CHAPTER 12

We were driving along Highway 1, just north of Big Sur, twisting around the tight mountain turns at around 35 mph, when the steering column in our car suddenly snapped. We immediately struggled to regain control and apply the brakes, as the vehicle flew wildly all over the road, like a epileptic pinball in the midst of a grand mal seizure.

Desperately trying to bring the out-of-control car to halt, we realized quickly — with widening eyes — that we were destined to fail, and the car went sailing right off the side of the cliff. Mind-blinding terror consumed our brain, as every muscle in our body contracted, and we prepared for our death. It seemed as though we heard the barely-audible voices of angels in a faraway realm singing sweetly to us, trying to pacify our terrified state of mind.

Time dilated, and everything moved in ultra slow motion, as all the significant events in our lives flashed by in rapid sequence. It seemed as though we hung in the air for an eternity, while awaiting the inevitable moment of impact. Our consciousness shifted and split as we flew through space. Some of us were very much in the driver's seat, experiencing every physical sensation, while others were deeply engaged in a vision on another plane of reality, begging God for life, and pleading for our continued existence.

The nose of our car was the first to hit, at around a hundred meters down the side of the mountain. The car flipped onto its back, fell right-side up again, and then rolled down another hundred meters or so, where a tree firmly set the car to rest. We were acutely conscious of the miraculous fact that we were alive, and that the car had finally come to a halt.

We looked in the rear-view mirror, expecting to see rivers of blood running down our face, and only saw our shiny white smile and bright green eyes looking as mischievous as ever. Unbelievably, we felt completely fine, and it seemed as though we were surrounded by waves of divine love.

We tried to open our door, and found that it wouldn't budge, so we climbed out the passenger side. We looked up around two hundred meters to the road above and couldn't believe that we were not only alive, but, although badly shaken, appeared to be virtually unscratched. Our car, however, was a total wreck. Feeling an incredible sense of overwhelming gratitude, we hugged the earth and kissed the sky.

We climbed up the mountain to the road, and when we reached the top, we turned and looked back down. It was one hell of a drop. Nobody goes over a cliff like that and just walks away, we thought to ourselves. We seriously considered the possibility that maybe we had actually been killed, that our body was still down there in the wreckage, and we were just a ghost wandering through the bardos, involved in some kind of post-death hallucination. Or perhaps our mangled body was down there still alive, and we were having an out-of-body experience. Everything was so dream-like, it was hard to tell what was happening.

We stuck out our thumb. Several cars passed by before a old clunky Volkswagen van, full of young college kids, stopped to pick us up and confirm our physical existence.

Fortunately, they were on their way to Santa Cruz, and we were extremely grateful for the ride. We'd deal with what was left of our car later. Nothing was more important at the moment than finding our way to Sari.

We told them about the accident, and how important it was that we get to Santa Cruz as quickly as possible. One of the kids offered us a puff of some ganja, but we declined, and sat quietly in the back of the van. We couldn't look out the window without getting dizzy and jumpy. With time we realized that we were in shock, and may have cracked a few ribs.

The flashbacks were extremely intense. As the kids debated philosophy and politics, we sat there reliving the experience — complete with muscle contractions — over and over. We tried to glean the elusive lesson to be learned from all this, wondering why had we been spared from the jaws of death. Perhaps the virus had protected us in some mysterious way, we theorized. The whole experience of losing control of our car and flying off a cliff — which couldn't have lasted more than a few seconds of earth time — brought all the significant aspects of our lives into sharp focus.

When they finally dropped us off at the Dominican Hospital Psychiatric Unit — totally traumatized, spaced, and disoriented — it was around 5:30 in the afternoon. According to a sign posted on the door — the visiting hours had just ended for the day. We rushed inside anyway, through the glass doors toward the reception desk to inquire about Sari's status. As we approached the front desk, the bright fluorescent lights glared down like angry evil spirits thrusting down psychic spears at us, and we were suddenly, without warning, grabbed viciously from behind.

"I got him! I got him!" the Cro-Magnon throwback yelled as we struggled to break free from his grip, but his hold on us was much too tight, and our ribs were hurting. His breath smelled like freshly-chewed raw meat, and we could feel his thick male member flush against our buttocks as he breathed heavily into our right ear.

"You like that, don't you, you little faggot," he said while grinding his cock against us. As his cold saliva dribbled onto our neck, we quickly considered our options, and decided it most appropriate to shout up to the reception desk for some kind of assistance, doing our best to make it clear that we were being attacked by an insane patient, a violent out-of-control lunatic on the loose.

"It's okay Freddy, loosen up and bring him over here," the bleached-white woman with red lipstick behind the front desk said coolly, completely lacking any emotional display whatsoever. What the hell was going on here? This, obviously psychotic, person behind us worked here? In the midst of the confusion, we realized there was something about that woman at the desk that we just didn't like. It was hard to pinpoint what it was exactly, but it had something to do with the fact that her face reminded us of the puckered-up ass on a baboon in heat.

"You're not getting away this time. I nearly lost my job because of you," Freddy griped at us. He continued grunting and mumbling obscenities from his 38 word vocabulary, as he dragged us, against our will, across the room. Our sneakers squeaked rebelliously against the white polished tiles.

"Welcome home Nicholas. We knew you'd be back eventually," said the nurse with a crookedly pasted clown smile, putting her index finger to her rectum-mouth, as she carefully examined us, like a detective searching for clues.

Our minds rushed in multi-directional confusion. "Hey, how do you know that name? What's going on here?!" we stammered.

Several young men appeared a moment later, and forcefully escorted us into a small sterile room with several uncomfortable-looking chairs. "Just doing our job," they told us. We were getting mighty pissed-off.

"Wait, Freddy, we have a special gift just for you," we said to our captor just before he left the room. We grabbed Freddy by the shoulders and kissed the bastard full on the lips, poking our virus-coated tongue briefly into his mouth. Yuck! He tasted like fermented pig mucus, but that will teach him to mess with us.

"Fucking queer," he yelled, slapping us to the ground, as we nauseatingly tried to spit his wretched taste from our mouth.

"Bon voyage," we said to him between gagging spasms, "May God have mercy upon your poor soul," we spit out, forcing the curved exposure of our front teeth into a facial expression reminiscent of a smile, cursing that son-of-a-bitch to the deepest bowels of hell.

Two female nurses, a male psychiatrist, and a pre-op (her bulge showed) transsexual social worker, sat in a row facing us. They spent several hours trying to convince us that we had escaped from this very hospital three months earlier. Reminding us that we suffered from multiple personality disorder and manic-depression, they claimed that this "Sari Feline" that we had come all this way here to rescue was simply one of our own alters, another personality sharing our brain — the one who planned and executed the escape that the rest of us weren't even conscious of.

We stared at the floor in disbelief. Could what they were saying possibly be true? We sincerely wondered about their theory, although it just didn't make any rational sense. The early pages of this book contain scenes which clearly demonstrate that Sari and Kato were simultaneously in different places. But we felt confused, after all we wrote those words ourselves, and they were just composed of only our own memories. Maybe the apparent separation was completely constructed in our minds? Perhaps we had been delusional all along.

But why should we trust these wicked people who were holding us against our will? Then again, who could we trust? We had no memory of being in the hospital, but then we weren't really sure. There were large gaps of missing time, and we began to question our sanity. Unsure of what to do next, we decided that it was high time that we inform them about the extraterrestrial virus, and our special status in the universe. But the psychiatrist must have been able to hear our thoughts, for he responded without our having uttered even a single word.

"Nicholas my boy, now think for just a moment, even if it's true, and you really are infected with an intelligent virus from outer space, shouldn't you at least question the critter's motives? How do you know this virus is as benevolent as it claims to be, or whether it really has your best interest at heart? Don't you think that you should at least be a little bit skeptical of the voices that you hear?" said Dr. Stanley Abraxas, our psychiatrist — a tall bearded chap with a British accent, receding hairline, and little round glasses. He spoke patiently, as though talking to a child, trying to gain our trust, and appeal to our logic.

A wave of intense paranoia washed over us, and our head began to swell with other people's thoughts. You see, being as swept away by her extra-galactic charm as we were, it had not quite occurred to us to question her motives. There was, of course, a possibility that the alien had deeper intentions than the "spiritually pure" ones that she shared with us.

But, although nature overflowed with examples of how many species will often deceive others for their own benefit, we couldn't even begin to see what Leticia was gaining from all this, that she wasn't giving back a thousandfold in her love for us. At this point we made a strong effort to stop broadcasting our thoughts, and constructed a psychic shield around our body so that no one could hear what we were thinking.

Dr. Abraxas told us that it was time we know the truth; the virus we had contracted before entering the hospital six months earlier was actually the result of a biological warfare experiment in a nearby military lab, that had escaped through an open sewage drain. Our having become infected with this maliciously-mutated, genetic material from the Devil's Workshop, he said, had seriously complicated our preexisting problems with MPD. The top-secret, CIA-crafted, hallucinogenic virus, he further explained, was psycho-mimetic, and had caused all of our personalities to become psychotic, one at a time, as the virus spread from personality to personality in our brain.

So the extraterrestrial personalities, then, were simply multiple hallucinations, manifestations of a virus-induced schizophrenia-like pathology, and all of their supposed communications with us were merely reflections of our extremely delusional state, or so he claimed. No, this couldn't be true. It just couldn't be. They must be trying to trick us; that's it we figured.

A thought crossed our mind. We considered kissing everyone in the room on the lips, quickly thrusting our tongue into their mouths, just so that they could experience the virus, and see the truth for themselves. But we resisted the impulse, slapping our hands to our head, discovering a quivering mass of squirming neural tissue between our fingers, screaming in horror, in a terror beyond terror, after which we strangely began laughing in hysterical fits. You see, we just couldn't figure out what was real. We turned our head skyward in desperation, searching for divine inspiration.

Then it hit us. We reached into our pocket and pulled out the glowing transcendental object that we brought back with us from one of our inter-dimensional voyages. "Wait, look," we said while proudly displaying the self-rearranging object, "here's proof. Behold — the transcendental technology." Everyone stared at our hand, and to our astonishment, they saw nothing. We put the object back into our pocket, and took this to be further proof of their nefarious natures.

"Where have you hidden Sari?" we found ourselves suddenly demanding, growing ever more suspicious of their motives. Unable to restrain ourselves any further, we leapt up, kissed Dr. Abraxas on the lips, and in went the tongue. We did not like the way he tasted either; too lemony, too salty, kind of stale, and slightly moldy, but the deed was done.

"There, now we can see for ourselves who's crazy," we said to the good doctor. Just then we felt a small prick in the right cheek of our buttocks, and within seconds a wave of dizziness soon washed over us. A high frequency buzzing, and what sounded like the monotonous repetitious clanking of heavy machinery, began to drown out their voices.

We felt a warm hand gently touch our shoulder, attempting to comfort us, and as we closed our eyes, their voices seemed to be drifting further and further away. The hospital room wavered and dissolved, just like it always does during the dream sequences on all those corny television shows, leaving us with the self-transcendent realization that everyone there was only a projection, a cast of cleverly-crafted dream characters created within the confines of our own imagination. Dr. Abraxas, the nurses, and the social worker were all neurochemical constructions designed inside the reality studios of our head.

In fact, there wasn't anyone, anywhere, who was outside of us. Everyone — Kacia, Leticia, Sari, Daimon, Kato, Willard, Ginger, the whole family of humanity included — was really inside our own mind. An exploding hush of voices was heard round the planet, as the rushing whirlwind of humanity's collective experience filled our mindscape with thoughts and feelings from people the world over. From the center of centers, one can see out through every single I in the Kingdom of United Verses.

At this point we divided, a force splintered us into polarizing fragments, and suddenly we encountered the Other. A winged alien superorganism with seven heads, each resembling Sari's in their own way, danced before us. Once inspected closely, we could see that she was actually composed of countless miniature individual beings, like a school of fish, or a perfectly synchronized flock of birds. A bright aquamarine aura of ethereal fire flickered about her for several meters, and we could clearly see, with microscopic detail, that this massive entity was composed of savagely hungry, virus-infected, multi-cellular creature colonies.

"Come to us," they sang exquisitely, like sirens, opening up their arms with seductive motions of invitation. They seemed to metamorphose from the body of a beautiful

Indian woman into a huge mammoth butterfly, gracefully flapping its large brightly-colored gossamer wings, in which hid millions of tiny faces, each whispering ancient secrets of existence to us. They glided towards us with the fluid grace of a troop of ballerinas dancing in the heavens among the stars.

We were terrified, and shrank back from them in eye-bulging, panic-stricken fear. "Stay away from us. Don't come any closer!" we screamed, as they continued to advance forward with all their shimmering glory, and their endless promises of eternal rapture, life everlasting, and infinite salvation.

We were absolutely petrified, frozen in a kind of para-physiological paralysis, yet we were paradoxically shivering with irresistible attraction, trembling with eager antici-pation, as they flew closer and closer to us. Completely mesmerized, and totally unable to react, we sensed that this was really it, whatever that meant. "Come, my dear Nicholas. Don't be afraid," they said sweetly, perfectly imi-tating the voice of our mother.

"Is it death that you're afraid of?" they asked, laughing afterwards like an old friend from our childhood. Then they started to present their selves to us sexually, in the very ways that we knew in our perverted minds turned us on most of all. Our nervous system felt completely naked. This creature seemed to know every innermost recess of our brain.

Immersed in a brain-shattering state of absolute mind-screaming terror when they finally reached our, now quiv-ering, gelatin-like form, we felt them sweetly kiss our fore-head with utmost tenderness — the lips of an infant — during the penultimate embrace. We started to cry, tears swelled and burst in our eyes, and our mouth dropped open.

As their slippery tentacles slithered around, and slowly surrounded our vulnerable embryonic form, we finally began to surrender to their all-consuming vibratory rhythms. As the bliss, the rapture, the ecstasy began to intensify, we clenched tightly onto their morphing, extracoporeal webbing; undulating flesh, composed of a higher dimensional blend of thought, matter, and love.

Dazzling crystalline patterns of intricate complexity grew out of her eyes and filled the entire cosmos. The patterns branched together into a massive organic complex, which was breathing, throbbing, and strangely composed of geometrically-organized arrangements of angels, devils, mythological creatures and archetypal figures. Some were strung together hand in hand, others were genitally-intertwined in various ways, displaying unusual caricatures of humanity.

They rose up majestically into the star-filled sky, as a purple vortex of unformed energy swirled below us, forming a tantric circus choir of smiling divinities and grimacing demons. The creatures sung harmoniously together, in perfectly-balanced, synergistic chorus. They grew up and outwards, like giant flower petals from the top of our head, as though we were in the center of a colossal, ever-blossoming botanical explosion, stretching upwards into infinity.

We looked deeper into the creature's fiery Mandlebrot eyes, watching karmically-charged scenes from our lives unfurl like animated fractals in fast motion — a frenzied carnival of chaos — morphing into a larger, previously unrecognized pattern that was somehow more us than us, our spirit ever-more distilled to its alchemical essence. Then it was all over in a single, blinding, all-consuming flash. Everything burst into a brilliant, all-revealing, clear-white light of love and truth.

We found ourselves alive and aware, but time appeared to have completely stopped, and space expanded far beyond human comprehension. We couldn't seem to distinguish our form, or any form, as boundaries with any solidity were impossible to perceive. Everything just blended into everything else. Our morphological interface with the universe had been completely reformatted, so as to be more compatible with the Intergalactic Internet, and we were liberated into a new order of seemingly boundless mystery. There is something to be gained from every loss, we realized. For the first time in our lives, we finally felt free.

A miracle in action. A glorious time to be alive in the universe. Pulsars and quasars winked rainbows knowingly at us. Nodding nebulae slowly drifted by, as we sailed — in all of our wonderful magnificence — across the vast oceans of interstellar space. Leapfrogging from star to star, we had become a tiny twist of hungry-to-replicate DNA, scanning for the appropriate evolutionary message — a certain sexy chemical signal — like a bee searching for that all-attractive flower with just the right shape, texture, scent, and precise molecular pollen configuration. We longed to satisfy that deep instinctive yearning for the delicious union of cosmic comet sperm with planet egg.

Steady as she goes. We steered our way through the stars. New horizons opened up in grand display before us, somewhere deep inside what, at one time, was the organic temple of Nicholas Fingers, sitting comfortably now with vacant eyes, in a small, dimly-lit and softly-padded cell; protected, safe and nourished. From within the designer-styled protein-coat of a freshly-birthed genetic intelligence, we surfed our way across the interstellar gravitational waves of the galaxy, completely at one with the entire universe, the spreading ripples of our own mind.

CHAPTER 13

We awoke abruptly, and discovered ourselves to be curled up tightly in a fetal position on an uneven rubber floor. All of our muscles were aching, and we felt as though we were locked up in the deepest dungeon of the Bastille. Schizophrenia sometimes carries with it a very distinctive odor, and we could smell the strong stench of psychosis in the air. We slowly stretched out our body, letting each joint crack in sequence, and then heard a gentle rustling sound coming from above. Quick as a neural impulse, our feline ears suddenly twitched to attention. Through the small air vent near the ceiling, the rustling grew steadily louder, and then, after a moment of silence, came a soft voice.

"Kato, are you down there? Can you hear me? Oh Kato, please answer me," the familiar female voice whispered, "It's me, Sari."

"Sari," we answered in disbelief, "is it really you?"

"The one and only — in the blood-and-spirit-filled flesh — at your service," she replied.

"But they told us that you were... That is, that we were...," we began in confusion.

Just then Sari pushed the metal grating out of the wall and stuck her head through. We couldn't believe our eyes. Sari had been crawling around in the hospital's ventilation system.

"Never mind what they told you. I've come to liberate you. I'm your savior, and I'm here to set you free," she said. "Now, c'mon we've got to get out of here and fast. Hurry up and give me your hand," she said reaching her arm down towards me.

We grabbed hold of Sari's hand, and, with her help, began scaling the padded wall. Sari clumsily yanked us up into the tight cramped metal tunnel. It was hot and dark inside, and one could only fit by lying flat and crawling like a worm burrowing through the earth. There were all kinds of eerie strange sounds reverberating down into wherever this mysterious passageway led.

We immediately kissed Sari deeply on the lips, and blissfully savored the sweet tangy taste we had so longed for.

"Let's go," she said breaking off the euphoric kiss about two hours too soon, "we don't have much time. Follow me." Since she was facing me, she had to move backwards for around fifty yards or so. We continued trying to kiss her face as we wiggled forward, until we came to a slightly larger area where she was just barely able to twist and turn her body around.

The tunnel narrowed as we wiggled along slowly behind Sari, and then it widened again. Most parts of the tunnel were only wide enough for us to crawl along on our hands and knees. As we followed behind Sari, she would purposely stop and bump her big butt into our face every so often, and giggle. Her female scent was especially powerful. Sari's wiggling tail turned our thoughts to ancient civilizations and early primate religions as we continued forward. We crawled through a winding labyrinth of twisting metal tunnels that seemed to continue for miles. One could spend whole lifetimes lost in here, as the tunnels branched off like fractals in all directions.

After about thirty minutes of crawling and wiggling through the dark, we finally came to a bright light, which stung our mole eyes like a spray of hot needles. We had reached our destination. Sari maneuvered herself up to the metal grating, stopped, watched, and waited for a few minutes in silence. The thumpa-thump-thump sound of our heartbeats became deafening, echoing down the tunnels, spreading throughout the ventilation complex, intermixing with all the eerie clicks, whirls, and humming reverberations. We felt a small mammal, with pointed little toes, run over our legs, and we let out a shriek.

"Shhh," Sari whispered, "we have to be extremely quiet." We waited in silence for several more minutes, until whoever was down there left. "Now," she suddenly said, pushing out the metal grating, "let's go." Sari slid, rolled, and fell on to the floor with a loud thump. We followed, landing on top of her, and discovered that we were now in the laundry room. Washers and dryers whirled around us. The smell of bleach and detergent tickled our nose, making us sneeze out our soul into the air. We caught it quickly with our left hand, and sucked it back in through our mouth.

Sari moved cautiously toward the door. After she checked to see if the coast was clear, she signaled for us to follow her. Up the stairwell we went, two steps at a time, until we reached a door at the top which led out to the parking lot, the promised land. We burst outside into the bright sunlight. Ah, sweet freedom sang like a choir of angels into our ears.

"Yes!" Sari exclaimed, making a fist and pulling it down and towards her chest. "Now, where's your car?" she asked.

"No car," we answered, feeling a shudder of remembrance travel up our spine.

"Oh, that's just great! Okay, we'd better run for it then, and get the hell out of here before they notice that we're gone," she said.

"Oh no you don't," the ape-like brute said as he grabbed Sari from behind and held her.

"Let me go you creep! Let me go right now," Sari yelled, as she struggled vainly to break free. "Kato," she yelled, "help me!"

"Oh, come off it Sari," the ape creature said, "How many times must I tell you. There is no Kato. There is no Nicholas. You're just hallucinating again. Now stop with the fantasies, and come inside for your Thorazine."

"No, I will not. You're wrong. He was just here. I swear it. Kato was just with me," Sari cried, looking around at an empty parking lot, "He was in Nicholas' body, which was right here just a moment ago. This just can't be. Kato? Where are you Kato? Where did you go?"

"Come now Sari, your doctor is waiting for you. You know that you only make it more difficult for all of us when you resist our efforts to help you," he said, tugging her towards the door.

"But he was just here. I swear it. He was right here. You've got to let me go. The whole world is in danger, and we have the tools to save it. Please, you've got to listen. You've got to believe me," Sari continued as the primitive primate carried her inside, kicking and screaming, through layers and layers of doors, and into Dr. Demovitch's office.

Dr. Lavinia Demovitch, an elderly lady with white hair and grey eyes, hastily reminded Sari that she suffered from a severe form of schizophrenia, and that Kato and Nicholas, like Daimon and the virus from outer space, were all long-term, on-going hallucinations that she had been having for many years. Sari didn't say a word, and just sat there staring with large vacant eyes. These people couldn't touch her; they couldn't even get close. Behind her eyes, and between her ears, she was safe.

Dr. Demovitch walked over to Sari and, with great compassion in her heart, reached down into the top of Sari's head with her right hand. With a quick jerking motion, she pulled out Sari's brain, and while shaking the grey dripping mass in front of her face said, "Sari, will you just look at this mess! This is your brain for Christ's sake! Would you look at it. See, the connections are all wrong. Everything is all screwed up. No wonder you can't think straight."

"Yuk," she added as she let it drop back into Sari's head, splashing blood, cerebral spinal fluid, fantasies, dreams, memories, and hallucinations all over the room. Sari was completely unfazed by this whole display. She didn't even flinch once, and just sat there, staring blankly, letting it all run down her face without so much as moving a muscle.

"All right, enough of you then," the doctor said, signaling the robot-apes outside the door over to pick her up and take her away. They moved Sari out into the dayroom, and placed her in her favorite chair, where she just sat and continued staring for several hours.

After several false awakenings, we suddenly came to and realized what was happening. It was hard to grasp it all at first, but once we understood that we had been traveling around in circles, and remembered who we really were in the Clear Light of Creation, why everything else just fell right into place rather quickly.

We just had to laugh at ourselves. It was time to rejoice, we thought, as celestial music set the stage for dancing through the higher spheres. Our masterfully self-crafted deceptions and delusions vanished the moment we awoke and rubbed the sand out of our eyes.

We looked up and there was Sari sitting across the day-room from us, radiantly beautiful as a butterfly preparing for flight. And how simple it all was. We exchanged smiles with Nicholas, who was sitting to our left, and closed our eyes for a moment, letting our minds drift free.

We slowly opened our eyes to a crimson sky, realizing that the scene had completely shifted. We found ourselves now seated on the edge of a mountain cliff in Maui, looking out over a lush green valley, through mist and rainbows, into the cobalt blue Pacific, where dolphins and mermaids slid effortlessly through the waves.

Sari sat by our side, and we smiled at each other as our eyes met. Sari winked at me, and we both laughed, as hundreds of tiny bright red hearts flickered between us like fireflies engaging in a wild dance of passion. Tumbling and crashing waterfalls hissed a fine spray into the air, which tickled our face like a million tiny kisses.

An endless array of magnificent flowers were in full blown around us. Birds were singing, and the warm moist air smelled sweet as ripe pineapples. Fairies and pixies fluttered about us playfully with the butterflies. We put our arm around Sari, and she leaned her head softly on to our shoulder, as our souls merged together. From this new perspective, I watched as the sun set in brilliant kaleidoscopic display over the rolling tropical sea.

ABOUT THE AUTHOR

Photo by Miriam Joan Hill

David Jay Brown is the author of *Brainchild* (New Falcon Publications, 1988), and is co-author of two volumes of interviews with some of the most fascinating people on the planet: *Mavericks of the Mind* (Crossing Press, 1993), and *Voices from the Edge* (Crossing Press, 1995). His work has been translated into Japanese, Dutch, Spanish, German, Italian, and Czechoslovakian. David holds a master's degree in psychobiology from New York University, and currently writes for publications all over the globe. He is working on a book about the unexplained powers of animals with British biologist Rupert Sheldrake, and maintains an award-winning Web site:

www.levity.com/mavericks

Also By David Jay Brown

Brainchild

David Jay Brown
Introduction by Robert Anton Wilson

Introduced by Robert Anton Wilson

A Neuroscience Fiction novel from the best-selling author of *Mavericks of the Mind* and *Voices From the Edge*. Hot, sexy and futuristic, this wildly erotic dizzily dazzling carnival ride explodes with the force of 4.5 billion years of evolution. Guaranteed to liquefy and reform any brain with courage enough to venture into its depths.

Told through the eyes of an immortal, perpetually young, erotically-minded rock-n-roll visionary, *Brainchild* is the story of how dreams, via nanotechnology, can become realities. Guaranteed to blow your mind.

"David Jay Brown writes like Walt Whitman on acid. He remembers his psychedelic experiences better than any other writer."
— Robert Anton Wilson, author of *Cosmic Trigger*

"A book I really enjoyed! Fascinating... *Brainchild* is on the far edge of cyberpunk."
— Timothy Leary, Ph.D.,author of *The Game of Life*

"That our perfected selves whisper to us from the future is but one of David Brown's fertile insights."
— Terence McKenna, author of *The Invisible Landscape*

"David is an ECCO agent. His writing is fantastic."
— John Lilly

ISBN 0-941404-92-7